PETE HEYSEN has cool...

former disc-jockey on Station 2FX in the
frenetic world of Australian radio-journalism,
Heysen became host of the *Crime Report*
show on TNTV.

Pete was climbing up and up. Too bad
when a beautiful corpse went to sleep
in his bed. On holiday too. In Honolulu.

No, thought Pete: the cops just wouldn't
understand. When they put those
plastic garlands round your neck in
Honolulu it can feel just like a noose.

Never Die
in Honolulu

Ian Hamilton

A Mayflower Paperback

NEVER DIE IN HONOLULU

Ian Hamilton

Mayflower Paperbacks are published by
Mayflower Books,
3 Upper James Street, London, W.1.
Made and printed in Great Britain by
Hunt Barnard & Co. Ltd., Aylesbury, Bucks.

Never Die in Honolulu

Chapter 1

The next time you find a dead girl in your Honolulu hotel room, what will you do?

Call room service for a casket? Check her for gold teeth? Pause to reflect, casually, on her naked beauty?

Or would you have the operator connect you with the Honolulu Police Department?

I decided against the Honolulu Police Department. I'm sure they're a genial and hospitable lot, but they are, after all, cops; and cops are embarrassingly logical men with a persistent belief in a cause for every effect, a killer for every killing.

I knew something about cops, enough to be certain that if I didn't soon wrench my eyes away from that slender young body draped face-up over the twin bed – tossed there as disinterestedly as a discarded beach towel or a pair of old sox – I would quickly become the cops' prime suspect and whatever your taste that's no way to enjoy a holiday.

Not that I'd reckoned on being involved in anything as spectacular as murder when I arrived in Honolulu. Something a little romantic, perhaps – something a shade different in the way of exotic pleasures – but I hadn't seriously planned on sharing a twin room with bath at the Reef Hotel with a well and truly dead darling.

I'd had more than one man's share of murder and madness in Sydney. But crime is like stinkweed or old mullet gut; it follows you about for a long time.

It had, it seemed, followed me five thousand miles across the Pacific.

Yesterday I had stood at the airport with a plastic lei around my neck and a free paper cup of pineapple juice in my hand, and the flashbulbs had popped. Next morning my picture was in one of those breathless newspapers they print for the tourists.

"AUSSIE TV MAN HERE," it said, and the caption told how my show in Sydney had recessed for Christmas and I had flown to Honolulu to have a break for two weeks.

The caption told, in its own effusive way, that I, Peter Heysen, hosted the show *Crime Report*, a weekly documentary live-and-film program devoted to crime, criminals and their victims. The picture showed a tallish character a little more battered than he should be in his late thirties, with a square face, dark hair and a large nose . . . looking a bit ridiculous with plastic flowers around his neck.

I wasn't to know then that another man in a fancy suite in another hotel on the island was also looking at the picture, pondering his own thoughts.

The newspaper said I had come for a rest and they were about right; I was tuned to expect phone calls in the night, informing me of a murder and expecting me to be on the scene in twenty minutes and meet the film crew there; I was tuned to listen to the pauses and inflections in a cop's voice, seeking the innuendo and the slip of the tongue; I was tuned to find news or to create news where none had existed.

Just as the editor of a Sunday tabloid prays for Saturdays generous with rape and train crashes, so the host of an hour-long Tuesday night crime bulletin purporting to be a public service waits nervously every Tuesday for a bold bank robbery, a gangland killing or the crushing of an old lady's skull by a group of juveniles. Healthy, wholesome family viewing can be an arduous business to sustain.

I happily, therefore, wasted my first morning lying on the beach, digging my toes into the sand, feeling the events of a long year slip from my mind.

I watched the big surf beyond the reef and the big American girls sporting nearby without much immediate desire for either; it was rest I wanted now, recuperation later.

The wide white arc of Waikiki beach, the monolithic hotels, the extravagant gardens and the swaying palms . . . it was all there, larger than the colour folders and more lavish than their desperate prose; every bit as grand as Hollywood might have done, had it had the chance to do it over, if it hadn't already.

Maybe it had. Waikiki beach, after all, was a sizeable piece of landscaping, the sand all being trucked in constantly from miles away. But perhaps that's how it goes when you want a simple island life.

I lunched quietly in a place by the beach, then I bought some shirts – orange and ultramarine and green with red swirls and violet splashes and tangerine palm fronds; they would

8

help me melt into the fluorescent scenery and become yet another tourist.

I drifted onto the terrace of the Moana Hotel, right on the beach by a banyan tree, for a lone drink and a look at the girls, for I reasoned that by tomorrow I would be refreshed and in need of company.

One girl in particular was worth a lingering moment: a tall girl, brunette with long brown limbs and big brown eyes and round brown glands high where a lady's glands ought to be, lightly held in a yellow bikini. She wore a hat, a straw basket affair with "UTAH" spelt out in mauve flowers. She was with a man who had big ears and he was paying for their drinks with cash, and I noted him only because it's a rare treat to see a traveling American use money instead of his Bank Americard.

But my attention returned to the mid-west, traveling from Utah to her toenails and slowly back up again, a pleasant little trip suddenly broken by a man's voice:

"Hi there, mind if I join you?"

He had approached soundlessly and now he was beside me, conspicuous in that brightly-plumed tourist crowd because he wore a London-cut lightweight grey suit with a blue wool tie and a big frangipani in his buttonhole. He moved into centre frame, right between me and Miss Utah.

"I'm sorry," he smiled, "I guess I just don't enjoy drinking alone, and I saw you here alone . . ."

His accent was American with a trace of something else: a rich, deep voice. He was tall, at least as tall as me, with a tanned face and blond hair. Danish-American? He might have been close to forty-five, yet his face showed hardly a line of age.

"My name's Max Rolfe." He grinned. "If you'd prefer me to just go away . . ."

Miss Utah was still out of view. I smiled back at him. "Join me," I told him. "Mine's Peter Heysen."

We shook hands and he sat at my table and waved down a waiter with the casual confidence of a man accustomed to instant service. "You're British?" he asked.

"More or less. Mostly less these days. I'm Australian."

"I've never had the pleasure but I hear it's a great country."

"I hear pretty much the same about America now and then."

The waiter came and we both ordered scotch.

"You staying here long?" he asked me.

"A week or two. It depends."

9

"Depends on the action, huh?"

I closed my eyes. "If she's about five-six or eight with a trim figure . . ."

"Big or small?"

"Rounded," I said. "Firm."

"Ah."

"With," I continued, "full hips, a sweet mouth and a sense of humour."

"And a free night?"

"And not too greedy," I added, opening my eyes again.

"It's all this sun and healthy island air," he said. "Makes a man a little eager. How long have you been here?"

"Twenty-four hours."

"You arrived eager. That your only reason for being here?"

His voice had changed almost imperceptibly as he asked the question.

"Do I need a better reason?"

"No. I guess we all need a break some time."

I told him, "It's been a long year, I came here to put it out of my mind."

"What business are you in?"

"Television. I have my own program."

"How about that? I'm drinking with a celebrity! Anybody around here know that?"

"I hope not."

He looked at me more closely. "I read about you someplace. Peter Heysen, you said? Now hold it – I'll get it – a crime program, right?"

"Where'd you hear that?"

He laughed. "I've got a great eye for faces. Saw your photograph in *The Islander* this morning."

"Tourist newspaper?"

"Sure."

I remembered how the picture had been one of dozens in the same paper, just another sleepy traveler getting off a plane. "They interviewed me out at the airport," I said. "I didn't think they'd run it."

He smiled. It was a big smile. "Peter, I've got an idea. You're in television, does the name David Davidoff mean anything to you?"

I shook my head.

"He's a vice president of NBC. You've just got to meet him,

a really great guy, David. He has a party in his lanai tonight. It'll be some party, they always are. You come. Don't argue with me, you hear? I'll call David and he'll invite you."

"That's very kind of you, Max."

"You want action, you just leave it to me."

"Girls?"

"Lots of girls, lots of girls."

"All this and David Davidoff as well. Thanks a lot."

"You're welcome. Anything for an Australian visitor. Stay here, I'll go call David right now."

He flashed another of his smiles and left me hurriedly and I watched him go, I watched his sure athletic walk, the loose swing of his arms, and I wondered if I could take him if it ever came to knuckles. It had to come to something: he wasn't setting me up for a ten dollar touch.

I decided to try and avoid open conflict. He might dress expensively and have many of the airs of wealth but he had the walk and, more importantly, the cool eyes, of a hardened street fighter. He might never have punched his way out of a kerbside brawl in his life, but I believed I could sense that he had all the necessary inclinations. He was quite possibly as dirty a fighter as me.

The waiter came with our glasses. I paid him and asked, "That gentleman who's with me, do you know him?"

"Sir?"

"The character who walked over and parked himself at my table – do you know him?"

"That's not my department, sir."

All waiters have the same mother. I peeled a note out of my wallet and placed it on the table. The currency was unfamiliar to me but he happily volunteered to accept it.

"His name is Rolfe, sir."

"I know that much already. He's a regular at this hotel?"

"I've only worked here going on two years – I guess he's stayed here maybe four times since I been here."

"Loaded?"

The waiter raised one eyebrow slowly. I asked, "He's flush, he's got money?"

"I guess he's got all a man would need, sir."

"What's his business?"

The waiter grinned slowly. "I don't know how he makes it but I can sure tell how he loses it."

11

"How ?"

"Women, sir. Always a different woman."

"Con-man ?"

"We never had any trouble with him here, except maybe with some girls on the staff. Sure wish I knew how he does it."

"Standing up, perhaps ?"

"No, sir, I tried that."

"How long has Rolfe been here this time ?"

"Just on a week. He came in from London. Leastways, that's what the hotel dick told me."

"Hotel dick ?"

"That's all he told me. Hotel dick isn't a great buddy of mine, he lives way outside my income bracket."

I put a small handful of money on the table and it disappeared.

"Room service was up in his suite, opening his luggage, and he saw a gun in his pyjamas so he told Bronson, that's the hotel dick. Bronson talked to Rolfe about it, asked him why he's carrying a .38 with his electric shaver. Rolfe said he was worried about something."

"He doesn't look a worried man to me," I said.

"Rolfe is what you might call an international playboy, sir. Not exactly jet set, kind of a loner for that, but the way he lays them he'd always have a smile on his face. Anyways, that's what he told Bronson – he was worried."

"Somebody's husband ?"

"He wasn't telling. Bronson said there'd be police trouble if Rolfe didn't check his gun at the desk. There's laws about that in the Fiftieth State, but Bronson said to check it at the front desk."

"So Rolfe handed in his gun ?"

"Yes sir. He was mad about it, said a lot of hard things to Bronson, but Bronson's a hard man himself. So Rolfe gave it to him and asked for all the protection that Bronson could give."

I put my hand on my wallet again. "You don't know what Rolfe is scared of ?"

"I sure wish I could help you, sir."

"I'll bet. Okay, thanks."

"You're welcome."

Max Rolfe returned to join me, smiling easily. He sat down and thanked me for the drink. "It's all fixed," he told me and I wondered just what he meant by that. "Be there around six," he said. "Davidoff's lanai, along the beach from here." He told me how to get there.

"Thanks, I look forward to it."

"Good to have you aboard, Peter Heysen." He raised his glass.

I raised mine and wondered just what it was that I had got aboard. My own unhealthy inquisitiveness had let me be suckered into something and had I known then that it would involve a dead girl before morning I'd have pulled out on the first plane.

Max Rolfe and I sat and talked for an hour and he arranged his pattern of questions to find out as much about me as he could.

And as we talked Miss Utah stood up to leave and the man with the ears watched her undulating departure with an expression of such total longing that I couldn't make out why he stayed on drinking alone at the table next to us.

Chapter 2

It was a very smart cocktail party. The hostess was on her ear in the first hour. Vodka and orange.

She was a sweet lady with an abrasive American accent from down south of the sinus; the drunker she got the funnier she got and I wasn't surprised to learn she was a retired comedienne and rehearsing alcoholic. A big blonde country girl with a big bawdy laugh and breasts like twin Edam cheeses. Bad sunburn.

Her husband on the other hand was born twenty years before her and, big brotherly, he watched over her with a smile, mopping up after her, chuckling softly at her raucous humour, shaking his head in silent wonder. He was a brightly polished man, almost hairless, with the steady but silent gaze, the impeccable manners and the slightly awesome air of toughness that belongs with a forty-fifth-floor executive.

Later, much later in New York, I met several like him in the deeply carpeted suites of the broadcasting empires; deliberate men, totally self-assured, all with fine skin that shone like ripe, hand-rubbed peaches. Somebody told me it was the air conditioning.

The Davidoffs were on vacation and they were making the most of it. They had taken a large lanai – a sumptuous apartment, decorated with Easter Island heads, some very good Gauguin copies, soft chairs in bright colours, and a rich blue carpet up to here. There were several other lanais like theirs close by, all in a small park of green lawn and palm trees, decently separated from but close enough to the razzle dazzle and swift room service of a big hotel.

Max Rolfe was plainly a friend of Mrs. Davidoff, for she met him at the door with a bear hug and a ribald gag.

He greeted her husband briefly, tossed my name at Davidoff almost as an aside, then launched himself again at Mrs. Davidoff, hooting with laughter, chasing her into another room on a loudly announced errand of indecent assault.

Davidoff, smiling happily at his wife's shrieks of obvious delight, led me into the party. Upwards of sixty people had spread themselves over three music-soaked rooms of the Davidoff lanai and, Davidoff said, there were more to come.

Innumerable young Hawaiian girls in bright dresses –the immense folds of the traditional muu muu had, promisingly, given way for the mini-skirt – hustled food and booze.

Davidoff was an excellent host, the kind who can spot an empty glass or a faltering conversation from one room to the next. Before I knew it he had found me a scotch, talked shortly yet knowledgeably with me about the leader of the communications kingdom for which I worked back home, and with some secret perception he had discovered my taste in women, introduced me to two of them, started a conversation, and then he had gone.

Unfortunately both the women were married and their husbands were with them, but it was a fast-moving party, mostly vacationing Americans who never move too slowly at the worst of times, and it very quickly became a happy blur.

I passed Davidoff on the run several times – once, with his wife, when she was dragging me firmly and with little protest towards the bedroom. Of course, we never quite reached the bedroom; I had the impression that nobody but Mr. Davidoff ever would. Mr. Davidoff had the same impression. He smiled and moved on. I liked Davidoff. His wife was a nut, she was fun, but I liked Davidoff.

Later, the party tumbled outside onto the lawns surrounding the Davidoff lanai, and food was conjured out of the hotel kitchens. The cocktail party had become a dinner party – a Hawaiian luau feast – and was soon to become an after-dinner party.

We squatted at low tables and ate a vast tonnage of island food, washed down with Verve Cliquot and accompanied by the throb and hum of the hula; four of the girls who had been serving inside now exchanged their mini-skirts for grass skirts and danced for us. Max Rolfe, drunk out of his mind by now, joined in. So did several others. So did I.

Then we sprawled in overfed groups, some standing about outside and more draped over chairs inside. I joined Max Rolfe and David Davidoff at the booze waggon that had been wheeled in under a palm tree.

Rolfe asked me, "How is it?"

"Some party," I told him and I turned to Davidoff. "Is it like this every night here?"

He laughed. "Don't think my wife isn't working on it."

"Great woman, your wife," Rolfe told him.

"I know."

"I'd steal her from you if I had half a chance."

"Max, I thought you had more important problems right now."

Max Rolfe grinned and looked at me. "My wife," he told me, "is married to a butcher."

"Let me get that right," I said. "Your wife is married to a butcher? Okay, what's the punch line?"

Davidoff said, "You're not playing straight man to him. He means it. His wife married again . . ."

"To a butcher," interrupted Rolfe.

"To the president of a meat-packing corporation."

"A butcher."

Davidoff said, "There's nothing wrong with Cunningham. I don't see how you could find a pleasanter man for your wife to marry." He glanced at me and his eyes were amused.

Rolfe threw back his drink, and when he spoke there was less amusement in his voice. "You can gig me about it, David, but Cunningham is a weak old fool. I'm going to get Elizabeth away from that s.o.b."

"Oh, come on, Max . . ."

"No David, I mean it. Look, how long have you known me?"

"Ten, say fifteen years." Davidoff turned to me. "Max divorced his wife for some unaccountable reason and ever since she married again he's wanted her back . . ."

"No," Rolfe said, "you get me wrong, David. I don't want her back, all I want is to get her away from that old fool Cunningham. He's twice her age or more and she's only a young woman. She's a little stupid in the first place, marrying him, but I'm going to get her away from Cunningham for her own good. Not for me. For her own good."

Max Rolfe was speaking in earnest now; drunkenly, but in earnest. Davidoff, the perfect host, noticed this swift change in his mood and set out to divert him.

"Well you know what you're doing, Max. I don't think it's any of your business, but it sure is none of ours. Anyhow, this is no place to argue it . . ."

Rolfe said, "There's things you don't even know about, David." And he looked at me hard and repeated it, "There's things you two don't even know about."

Davidoff gripped him by the elbow, as if to shake him from his sudden depression. "Meantime, before you do something about it, you don't feel partial to a little fun in your life? I mean, you haven't detected the high incidence of young ladies at the party. I don't even know where the hell they all came from, but I sure did notice them."

Max Rolfe looked about at the groups of people under the lanterns. He laughed gently, his thoughts plainly elsewhere. "Sure, sure. I talk too much anyway." And without another word to us he lurched off into the thick of the party.

Davidoff turned to the bartender to recharge our drinks. I asked, "Is he serious? Is he really going to try to get his wife back?"

"You heard him, Peter. He doesn't want her back. Least, that's what he tells us. He's heading for New York shortly. All he wants is to charge into the city on a white steed like some goddamn white knight and rescue her from her marriage to that fool Cunningham. Cunningham is a fool, you know. Wealthy man, successful, but kind of eccentric. I can't help agreeing with Max, I don't see how she could possibly be happy with him. She's a sensuous woman, all female, and only

16

thirty-two years old, thereabouts. Cunningham's in his seventies, he wouldn't bed her down too often. But what I don't see is how Max is going to do anything about it."

"Or why," I said.

Davidoff steered me towards a new group of people. "With Max," he said, "you'll never know why. He has his own reasons. Have you meet these folks over here? This is Tom Graves and Mary Graves from Indiana, this is Jerry Sleeman, he's from Los Angeles, I want you to meet Peter Heysen, he's from . . ." And the party was beginning to gather new life. Alka-Seltzer was handed around to the needy, the music started in loud, and the diners who had overcome their indigestion fell out onto the lawn to dance.

A warm tropical night with a full moon and no clouds. Food by the plateload, liquor by the crate, the music and the dancing, all produced a wildly pervading sense of to-hell-with-it-all. Two days in Honolulu and I was a new man; just as drunk as I ever got, which is about as drunk as a man can get, but it was a frantic new kind of intoxication. Always in the past there had been a reflex operating, an ancient sense of self-preservation deep down in my gut that had got me home or out of trouble or away from the sight of traffic cops. But this night, under these skies, in this place, it ceased to function.

Clarity returned now and then, as it is apt to do no matter how hard you belt yourself, and I found there were only a few of us left.

Our hostess was propping up a palm tree, relaxed in a beautiful sleep with half a coconut precariously balanced on her head. Our host, eyes half closed but still very much in command, stood talking quietly on the lawn with another man and two women. The whole group seemed to be swaying. In a dark patch under another tree, Max Rolfe was dancing and kissing and groping about stupidly.

I was dancing the leadfoot shuffle with a head of long, fine black hair snuggled into my chest.

I reached down, found her chin, pulled her head gently back so I could look at her face. She smiled, closed her huge brown eyes, made a kissing movement with her lips, pressed her body hard against me to keep me upright, then lowered her head again.

I couldn't recall if I had seen her at the party before or not, but I was smitten with instant love. I peered over her shoulder and saw she was wearing a bright mini-skirt and no shoes. While the temporary clarity remained with me, I decided it was time to head for home or some such place. A good party was approaching its happiest conclusion. Seduction time drew nigh.

Chapter 3

Max Rolfe and I walked along the dark beach with the two girls, tripping about in the soft sand, all four of us falling on top of each other, pausing every few yards for a fumble in the moonlight, then moving on.

At the Reef Hotel, we helped each other down concrete steps off the beach past closed shops and into the hotel carpark. We waved each other elaborately into an elevator.

We fell about in the corridor outside one of the rooms. The girl with me had the key. Max Rolfe and his girl, after a flourish of besotted farewells and good wishes for each other's comfort, left us to find their own room.

For a troubled moment I wondered what my girl's name was. Then the happy spirit of Hawaiian relaxation swept over me and I cared not. We tumbled into a large, pleasant room with a view down the beach to the lights at Diamond Head. She closed the drapes on the window and, in the light of one small bed lamp, slowly undraped herself.

It felt like a replay of the old gag: if I'd tried harder I might have had her.

And while we made love it occurred to me, in the odd way that such things do, that she must have been one of the hula dancers.

The love-making cleared my head. Now it was impossible for a gentleman to ask a lady what her name was. We stood up and, because it was dark and no windows faced ours, we stood together naked on the terrace and watched the moonlight spearing through the waves off Waikiki, feeling the breeze against our bodies. Then, of course, it had to happen:

The phone rang. I looked at her and she stared right back

at me and shrugged. I told her, "As well as I can remember, this isn't my room. You better answer it."

"It wouldn't be for you?"

"Who'd know I'm here? Somebody must know you're here."

"Only the front desk," she said. "They think I'm staying just overnight. I had to come in with a suitcase."

"Whose arrangement?"

"Mr. Davidoff."

"He's an excellent host. Answer it, for God's sake."

I stepped back inside and watched her cross the room un-selfconsciously in the semi-dark. She lifted the receiver, spoke three words, then told me, "It's for you."

"Who is it?"

"Max Rolfe. I think he's in trouble."

I took the phone and Rolfe said, "Peter? Max. I wasn't sure if I recalled that room number right. I got problems, old friend, and I need you right now."

"What is it?"

"The phones have many ears, friend."

The girl stood watching me, apprehensive. "Can't it wait till morning?" I asked.

"Peter – it's urgent. Please. I'm in 896."

"I'll be right there."

I put the phone down and groped for the light switch. The liquor had cleared even more now, the way it can when it must. "You're right," I said, "he's in some kind of trouble."

"What's happened?"

"You don't know?" I asked her.

"I don't know. Honest."

I found my sox and underwear and started to dress almost as quickly as I had undressed.

She said, "I don't want to be mixed up in anything."

"You'll be alright, you stay here."

"Yes."

"You stay here. Don't go away." I stopped pulling on my trousers. "Don't go away. We have the whole night. I'll be right back."

"Yes."

"Look, dammit . . ."

"I will wait."

"Okay then, okay." I scrambled into the rest of my clothes

19

and told her again, "Don't go away." She nodded and watched me go and already I knew that was the end of that night. The end of the fun part.

Chapter 4

I tapped on his door and Max Rolfe let me in. His hair was mussed up but he was fully dressed. He took me into the room, an almost exact replica of the room I had just been in, and on a replica of the bed I had so recently made love there lay a dead girl, but this was no replica, she was a real dead girl.

Nobody should ever die in Honolulu. Lying with a bad case of the horrors in Lower Slobbovia, perhaps; seasick and cold on an English pleasure cruise across the Channel, almost certainly; trapped in Paris with all your money gone, you might as well; but never, never under any circumstances should anybody ever die in Honolulu. It's too good to leave. I'm inclined to believe that nobody ever does.

Except, of course, with one nakedly obvious exception.

Rolfe stood quietly, watching me. He seemed stunned, as if deep down he knew it was all a drunken dream.

I asked him, "What the hell . . . ?"

"I fell asleep." He ran his fingers slowly through his tousled blond hair, his only visible sign of any emotion. Even his voice was flat and expressionless. "We had sex, then I went to sleep. I woke for more and there she was."

"But how the *hell* . . . ?"

"I don't know! I went to sleep is all I know! Do you think . . . maybe it was too much for her ? I mean, all that booze and everything . . ."

I switched on the harsh main lights in the room and went closer to look at her. She was dead, no question, yet at first glance it seemed there was no mark on her. I looked again, more carefully. I'd seen enough corpses in my time with *Crime Report* but rather than get accustomed to death, each time if anything I felt worse, a chill in the tripes.

I straightened up. "You're having me on, Max."

20

"How's that?"

"You reckon you don't know how she died?"

"I told you . . ."

"I'll tell you, then. She didn't just drop dead from an over-abundance of your charm and athletic ability. She was killed. Deliberately."

"Oh, come on, Peter . . . !"

"Max, she was murdered. Expertly, too. Did you move her at all when you woke up?"

"Move her! Jeesus, I shook her about a little, then I knew she was dead so I called you and I got dressed. How do you know she was murdered?"

"Just there, you can see the bruise on her temple," I said. "If you'd like to look . . ."

"No thanks."

"It's only a light bruise, very efficiently done. I'd say she died instantly. You have to know the exact spot. Too many people do these days. How good are you at karate?"

"Take a look at my hands, do you see any karate callouses there?"

"I believe you. Did you hear anything at all in your sleep?"

"I guess something woke me, maybe I did hear something. Nothing special that I can remember. Do you have to talk about it like it was a flat tyre or a horse broke its leg? You might be used to murder but this is a whole new venture for me."

"Then you better sober up, Max, you're in for a long night."

"Yeah. You're right. We call the police, huh — ?"

"What else would you do, Max? Just walk out of here?"

"I thought about it. It looks pretty bad for me."

"Why? You didn't have any motive, did you? I'll call them now, get it over."

"No, wait." He stopped me. "You forget, I know this town, I know the Honolulu cops. There's one in particular I know, he used to be on homicide detail. I want to call him personally."

"A man has a right to one friendly cop in his life," I said.

He approached the phone, then he paused. "Not through the hotel operator," he said. "It's going to take some explaining. You wait here, I'll call my cop friend on a pay phone outside."

I looked at him. I wasn't seeing too well: heavy drinking, loose sex and a lithesome dead body all in a matter of a few hours is a little hard on the mental digestion. I felt good and I wanted to believe him so I said, "Go and call the friendly cop."

"You'll wait here?"

Some facts take longer to hit you than others and murder is a fact that hits hard but takes some time to hurt. It was beginning to hurt him now.

"Okay," I said. "I'll wait."

He picked his sports jacket up off the bed and left quickly. I switched off the main lights and paced the room, my eyes constantly wrenched back into the pool of light thrown by the bedside lamp, a spotlight on a lovely dark-haired girl, the smooth lines of her body softened in the shadows.

Why does a man fall sucker to strangers? The smartest of us gets caught once in a while. But only the dumbest of us gets stuck in a hotel room with somebody else's corpse. And after twenty of the longest minutes known to man she was beginning to spoil my vacation and Max Rolfe was beginning to spoil my faith in human nature, which had never been overly enthusiastic at best.

And gradually it came to me through the folds of moronic fat surrounding my tired brain; it came to me as it must have come before to thousands of victims in thousands of con games. Rolfe had set me up.

Max Rolfe had left me holding the baby. Left me standing like a drunken half-wit in a strange hotel room with a cooling corpse not of my own making, with little chance of adequately explaining my presence to an overzealous or even a totally non-zealous cop. And I still had a couple of weeks of vacation left.

I thought back. I had touched the door handle and the light switch – no, only the light switch, Rolfe had opened the door for me.

And going out, Rolfe had opened the door himself, with his sports jacket in his hand. Had he used his jacket to avoid leaving his prints on the door handle?

Once suspicion begins it grows like a galloping tumor. I hadn't seen him touch anything since I entered the room; had he wiped it all clean?

But I was being too harsh on Max Rolfe, surely. It would, after all, take most of twenty minutes to hustle up his friendly cop. And when I heard voices in the corridor approaching the room I knew it was alright. He was back already; he was being unnecessarily noisy about it but at least he had returned. I stood up and went to the door, determined to talk my way out of this mess as quickly as possible.

The silence stopped me. There were no more voices, yet I knew they were there, standing just outside the door.

I didn't move. Nor did they. Why didn't Max open the door, had he lost his key ? Perhaps he hadn't taken it. Why didn't he knock ?

Somebody did. Very loudly. And somebody's voice, the voice of authority, called, "Open up in there, please. This is the police."

I backed off. I reached the light switch and smeared my prints on it with the cuff of my shirt. I could imagine them standing, backs to the wall and waiting to see if I would gun them down through the door with a hip-pocket cannon. I wished I had one.

No Max Rolfe. He had blown and left me to handle the police. I hurried to the floor-length drapes and behind them the wide glass doors that opened onto the terrace.

"Okay, we're coming in."

I slid open the glass doors, stepped out onto the terrace and closed the doors again swiftly as I heard the key going into the entrance door.

They had been outside holding a master key and I had been inside holding my breath. Now they were inside and I was outside on a narrow terrace nine floors above the darkness of Waikiki beach.

And I had come to Honolulu for a rest.

Chapter 5

Always trust and respect your neighbourhood police officer. That way lies law and good order in the community. But it's not to say that you should stand about and talk with the man when he's on duty. Best not to bother a cop when he's hot in pursuit of justice or whatever. And it's particularly true if the neighbourhood police officer in question comes from somebody else's neighbourhood.

I went over the terrace railing, lowered myself down quickly, swung then dropped onto the terrace below. I tried not to look down; from nine floors up, the soft Waikiki beach sand could come up like a slab.

Next time you're at the Reef Hotel in Honolulu – and that's a small treat you will of course allow yourself often – take note of the central corridor on every floor; it ends in a small terrace of its own, and the way around the wall from this small public terrace onto the private terraces on the same level is a simple process, you just lean out over the beach and step around the wall. No doubt a few party crashers and vacation romeos have tried it without trouble. This was one fugitive from embarassing official questions who managed it.

I sprinted along the darkened, quiet corridor to the elevator. The car that had dropped the police off at the floor above was still up there. I punched the button and waited, then went down in it to the fifth floor. Again I did a sprint down the corridor and back to the room where, not so long ago, in about the time it takes to commit murder, I had lain with a lovely Honolulu maiden.

But apart from the rumpled bed there was no sign to say that anyone had been in the room.

I checked quickly; she had closed and locked the big sliding glass door onto the terrace, she had emptied the ashtray – probably into the toilet – and she had left the door unlocked and the key in the middle of the bed.

I wiped my prints from the outside door handle, locked the door from the inside, then went slowly through the room, remembering all the things I had touched and wiping them clean with my handkerchief.

When I had double-checked, when I was certain I had covered everything, I switched out the lights and stood quiet and still in the dark room, listening. The extravagant wail of four sirens in bad harmony outside the hotel was all I could hear and all I needed to know.

The Reef Hotel in Honolulu is a fine hotel and a good place to stay, but on this particular night I'd had enough. It was time to get back to my own hotel for a peaceful, innocent sleep.

I looked down to the beach and spotted the first of the cops, his eyes fixed on the hotel. So then I took a walk – casually, trying to look like anybody's party guest – to the other end of

24

the corridor and I spotted more of them, down in the canyon between this wing of the hotel and the next.

I knew then that there'd be more in the carpark under the hotel, a tight group of them in the foyer, a couple on the service entrances and some on the roof and any other of the more convenient escape routes. I sweated a good deal behind the ears now. I hurried back to the room that I was coming to think of as my second home.

I left the lights off and stood in the middle of the room, smoking nervously, listening through the pores of my skin.

There was nothing to hear. And slowly I relaxed, realising I had been standing on the balls of my feet ready to spring when the shadows attacked. But the shadows were friendly, at least in this room for the time being.

I was smoking Australian cigarettes, a blend of the harshest varieties of Australian tobacco and one that would make it too easy for any half-active cop to trace me, so I sat on the cool tiles in the bathroom and dropped my ash in the toilet.

Item one, I was cornered by a bunch of cops who, because I was a stranger in the hotel and could not give any likely reason for being there, would connect me with their lately discovered cadaver.

Item two, I was indeed and in truth too closely connected to the deceased for my own comfort.

Item three, I had been set up as the bunny, the patsy, in a game whose rules I knew too well but whose definition or direction I was completely blind to.

If the cops had found me with any other body in any other place at any other time, I might have relied on their good intentions and given myself up – I just might have. But Max Rolfe had walked off and left me to be found with the dead girl and by the rules of the game there was no way I could be sure that was all he had done to make my life uncomfortable. If the Honolulu Police Department made me their guest for the night they might find untold horrors to confront me with by morning, all of Rolfe's making.

Problem one, then, was to escape, to find breathing space, to find Max Rolfe and to learn just what caper I'd been suckered into.

Problem two was to find out why.

Problem three, to clear myself. I settled down for a long night on the tiles.

25

One day, some learned egghead or hack journalist will write a worthwhile treatise on the psychology of waiting, that non-occupation which a man spends most of his life at.

Some wait forlornly for lottery wins, ships to come in and dogs to have their day. But infinitely more frustrated, more acid of stomach and suicidal of mind is he who stands forgotten in an airline standby queue, he who sweats it out in a dentist's waiting room, he who looks ridiculous outside the ladies' powder room – and it should happen to everybody – he who gets cramp of the Khyber Pass sitting about in dark Hawaiian bathrooms waiting for the sun to come up.

I stood and scratched and walked about the room. I ran out of cigarettes, my hangover ran its predictable course from an agony behind the eyes to a desperation in the throat that no tap water could soothe and still there was no dawn, still the cops suffered their own frustration of waiting down on the beach and, certainly, at every exit. It was a bad night for all of us. I heard them outside in the corridor a few times but obviously the hotel management had persuaded them not to go bursting into a few hundred bedrooms.

The dawn crept into the room by inches. I looked out through the drapes and saw the first handful of insomniacs and health nuts on the beach. Two of them stopped to talk with the cops and already the cops were looking embarrassed.

Soon there were more of them; some young kids out on boards to get the early surf, others running up and down the beach, and a man who walked in up to his ankles and stood there puffing at a huge cigar and, oddly, he had big ears. I finally pulled my eyes away from him and the cops had gone. I gave them another half-hour then cautiously left myself.

There were still two cops standing by the tours desk in the near-empty foyer. I had splashed my face with cold water and run a comb through my hair and I tried to look as perky as if I'd just stepped out of the shower. I had my jacket slung loosely over my shoulder and I kept my hand high to hide my unshaven face.

I tried to look like a guest. I glanced quickly at the man on the registration desk and told him, "Morning."

He flashed a hotelier's smile and said, "Good morning, sir. Looks like a good day."

"Sure hope so," I said, and I kept on walking, easy, casual, like a young millionaire who had just come down from his penthouse apartment. I didn't look at the cops but I could feel their eyes on me.

I walked faster now, past the small group by the car rental desk and out onto the street. Soon the hotel would swarm with people, the shops in the foyer would be crammed, and the cops knew it. They had missed their man and in the process I had probably missed mine. There was no telling where Max Rolfe might be by now.

At my own hotel I went to my room and showered and shaved and changed. I knew Rolfe wouldn't be there but I called his hotel anyway.

"I'm sorry, sir. Mr. Rolfe checked out early this morning."

"No forwarding address, I suppose?"

"No sir."

"About what time did he check out?"

A pause. "It must have been around five-thirty a.m. sir."

Chapter 6

I put the phone down. Where do you find an almost total stranger in an almost totally strange place?

I called David Davidoff.

"Oh, hi there Peter Heysen. You're up a little early, aren't you?"

"Aren't you, David?"

"Hell, I'm always up this hour. My wife, she'll surface around noon – tomorrow maybe." He chuckled. "Boy, she had herself a night. How about you, last I saw you were headed out with Max and two lovelies. A good night?"

"It was a good party, thanks David. You provided some interesting girls."

"Hell, I didn't *provide* them, Peter! Who'd need to in this town. They just happened!"

"They did? Tell me, have you seen anything of Max since we left the party?"

He thought about it. "Why do you want him so early? Was there some kind of trouble?"

"No . . ."

"With Max you never can tell."

"You haven't seen him, then?"

He laughed. "Peter, if you were in any trouble with Max last night, forget it. Max moves out fast when it suits him. You won't find him. He'll find you."

"Perhaps he will."

"Say – listen now – not real trouble, was it? I mean, just a fight or something – not big trouble?"

"No, nothing to worry about, David. I suppose he'll turn up."

"Sure. Yeah, sure he will. How about lunch today, Peter?"

"Thanks, I'd like that."

"Come around twelve, time for a few drinks, okay?"

"Okay."

"And if I see Max I'll have him call you."

"Thanks, David."

I tried the other major hotels but Max Rolfe hadn't checked in through the night. There were too many lesser hotels so I went down for breakfast and I sat in the sun on the terrace and ignored the sporting girls and poked at a pancake and thought about Rolfe. I didn't finish breakfast. I signed for it and left, and walked down Kalakaua Avenue, the main business street of Waikiki, and stopped off at the American Express office.

"Can you tell me what airlines fly out of here in the morning – from the very early morning right through till around now?"

"Surely, sir." She checked her files and folders and gave me the airlines.

"Fine, thanks."

"You're welcome."

There was no point in checking Max Rolfe with American Express or any of the other agencies, none of them would have been open. But the airport offices of the airlines would have been staffed.

I tried them one at a time. Airline people are among the most harassed in the world, especially in busy ports like Honolulu, and they get a little suspicious when you start asking for names of their passengers. I told them Max Rolfe was a friend of mine, I had urgent information about his wife, I asked could they help me?

I struck out with the first one but I made it with Pan Am.

28

The girl behind the desk riffled through papers on a big clip board and found the manifest for the early flight out.

"Yes, here it is, sir. Mr. Max Rolfe." She looked at me. "I remember him now, a tall man, blond."

"You'd remember him. Handsome and charming."

She smiled. "Oh, very, sir." She ran long fingers through her auburn hair. "Let's see . . ." she looked at more papers . . . "Mr. Rolfe was on our nine a.m. flight, that's flight 822, the through flight from Papeete, scheduled to arrive at L.A. at three fifty-five p.m. local. He was ticketed to connect with our flight 517, leaving Los Angeles about ninety minutes later, at five thirty-five p.m."

"Destination?"

"Rio de Janeiro."

"Great."

"Yes sir, I believe it is."

"What's your next flight out of here?"

"To the mainland?"

"Anywhere connecting with a flight to Rio de Janeiro."

"I thought you simply wanted to get a message to Mr. Rolfe, sir? We could contact him at our L.A. terminal or even in flight, if it's urgent."

I improvised. "Thank you, but I can contact him in enough time by cable through our business agents in Los Angeles. I'll let him know I'm following on. He'll want to see me personally."

"Of course." Again the smile, a lovable smile under any other circumstances. She ran a glossy fingernail down her flight schedule.

"You've missed 812. Our next flight to the mainland is flight 2, leaving at twelve noon through San Francisco . . . if you continue through New York I can connect you there with flight 203 to Rio."

"Can you get me a seat on that flight?"

"Just the one, sir?"

"Yes, economy if possible, first if absolutely necessary. I have to be on it."

"It's heavily booked to San Francisco but we may have an early cancellation." She went away and came back with good news. She wrote out the ticket and I paid for it with my credit card. The credit card people would all need transfusions when the account reached them.

"Thanks," I told her, "you've been very helpful."

"You're welcome, sir. Thank you for flying Pan Am."

I didn't have the heart to tell her I'd have flown strapped under the wing of a Tiger Moth to get out of Honolulu and close to Max Rolfe right now. And I knew I meant it when I walked out to find a cab back to my hotel and saw the headlines in the local press: "GIRL SLAIN IN HOTEL – EXPECT ARREST TODAY".

Chapter 7

If I'd stayed in Honolulu I'd merely have been in the way of the Honolulu Police Department, hampering their investigations; they could go about their affairs much more effectively without me underfoot. It was the only decent thing I could do, get out of Hawaii.

As soon as I could loosen my seatbelt I tilted the seat as far back as it would go, plugged the stethoscope gadget into my ears, tuned to the pop music channel and wound up the volume to drown out the fat lady from Chicago sitting next to me, and closed my eyes.

I tried to think about the past twenty-four hours: meeting Max Rolfe, then the party and its grisly hangover and Max leaving me to take it on the jaw when the police found me in a strange hotelroom with a dead girl.

There were too many obvious questions. Why had Max Rolfe set me up? Who was the girl? Who, indeed, was Jug Ears and did he fit in anywhere? Would I ever catch up with Max Rolfe and get any answers from him? Was he really headed for Rio de Janeiro after all? The press story hadn't helped me, it told me nothing I didn't already know better by experience. I doubted if I would ever get any answers.

I sat up for lunch and a brief informative lecture on hormone pills from the fat Chicago lady, then I reclined again with my ears plugged and my eyes closed against the in-flight movie, and I slept all the way to San Francisco.

From there through to New York I had a whole row of seats to myself; I pulled out the arm rests and spread my legs out and put my head on a pillow. Numbed by the monotone of the engines and the sensation of movement, I stared at the ceiling and made a decision.

There was no gain in going all the way to Rio. Max Rolfe could go to ground there or head on out for any place and eventually his trail must grow cold.

I recalled his drunken soliloquy about his first wife when we were at the Davidoff party; Davidoff had said Rolfe's wife was in New York and Rolfe would be going there shortly to see her, to persuade her to leave her second husband. Davidoff had convinced me that Rolfe was just mad enough to attempt it. And the more I thought about Rolfe the more I wondered if all my answers might not be waiting for me in New York. Max Rolfe himself might have stopped there already, his ticket south could have been a blind to put me off the scent.

I would stop off in New York and get to his former wife. At worst, it would keep me out of Honolulu.

It was early morning – a clear, cold, fresh morning – when I walked into the terminal at Kennedy Airport. I'd taken time on the plane to shave and freshen up and now I arranged a city hotelroom and a seat on the helicopter into Manhattan.

New York climbed up the sky at me and slowly spread itself out below me and I had the sensation of being swallowed as the helicopter lowered its passengers down into the gut of the great, grey city. We hovered a moment above the heliport, still high over the city and yet already below the level of the tallest buildings.

The moment I stepped out of the helicopter I knew I should never have left Honolulu; the cold clapped itself around me, jolting me with its sudden intensity. At least a Honolulu jail would have been warm. I rammed my hands into the pockets of my summer suit and hunched my shoulders against the bite of the wind.

I took a cab ride to my hotel, staring out and up at the tall forest of buildings, surprised and unprepared for the greyness of New York. Pedestrians in heavy topcoats hurried against the stinging wind that howled straight down whatever Avenue it was that I was on.

I sprinted into the sudden and glowing warmth of the hotel foyer, a foyer of plush and gilt, and the porter with my suitcase took me to the registration desk.

The polished, hair-slicked, ever-smiling man at the desk

was talking with another, a taller and better-built man with a coat over his arm, and with a suspicion born from long association I could smell cop. The shiny character behind the desk glanced quickly at him then flashed me a professional hotelier's smile.

"Good morning, sir."

"Morning. My name is Peter Heysen, I have . . ."

"Ah yes Mr. Heysen, we've been expecting you. Did you have a pleasant flight ?"

"Yes, thanks."

"Would you like to fill in this card ?"

The man with the coat was a cop, I was certain of it now; I could feel him scrutinising me as cop acquaintances of mine back home had done often enough. When I'd registered I turned to follow the porter and there was no great shock to my system when a quiet, deep voice stopped me:

"Excuse me, Mr. Heysen."

All innocence, I turned. "Yes ?"

"You're Mr. Peter Heysen from Sydney, Australia ?"

"How did you know that ?"

"I'm Detective Frank Pagnucco from the District Attorney's office."

"Well, it's nice of you to greet me . . ."

"You've just arrived from Honolulu ?"

"Yes. I wonder why. It's warm there, cold here." I managed a sickly little laugh.

"I'd like to take up a few minutes of your time, Mr. Heysen."

I propped myself casually against the registration desk. So casual, with all nerves ready for one almighty spring through the main entrance.

"Fire away," I said.

He looked around the busy foyer. "Maybe you'd prefer to talk someplace else ?"

"I see. Why don't you wait around while I get my gear into my room, then perhaps we could . . ."

He took me firmly by the elbow and led me after the porter with my suitcase. It wasn't so much that he was pushing me, it was just that he leaned a little hard, he was determined and he wanted me to understand that fact, and I understood perfectly.

"I'll accompany you to your room Mr. Heysen. We'll talk up there."

Chapter 8

The porter had been standing by the elevator, his Negro face a picture of total disinterest; as we approached, his dark eyes flicked across the cop and across me and up to a point somewhere near the ceiling and I knew that he, too, understood perfectly.

Once inside the elevator the cop released his grip on my elbow. The porter stood well away from us, about as far away as you can get in an elevator, and he carefully avoided looking at either of us. The car stopped and he all but ran with my suitcase down the long, silent corridor to my room.

He let us both in. It was a big, comfortable room with a wide view of the city.

The cop, without seeming to move more than one or two minor muscles, slipped a dollar into the porter's hand, eased him out of the room, and closed the door. The cop then stood by the door with his hands in his pockets, his coat slung over his shoulder.

"That was very kind of you," I said. I smiled my most televised smile. "I didn't know my old friends in the New South Wales Police Department had alerted anybody to greet me."

It had seemed a good line but I realised immediately it was a tactical error.

Detective Frank Pagnucco of the D.A.'s office said, "Oh, you're known to the police in Australia, are you?"

So I stopped my idiotic smiling. I walked to the window and lit a cigarette. "They know me because I work with them."

"How's that, Mr. Heysen?"

"I have a television program, it has to do with crime. Look, this isn't amusing any more, what's it all about?"

He watched me for a moment then he tossed his coat onto the bed and came to the window to join me.

He said, "I believe there was a little trouble in Honolulu just before you left?"

"Trouble?"

"The D.A.'s Office had a call from Honolulu. They traced

33

your flight and they knew you'd pass through here en route to Rio de Janeiro. They asked us to have a talk with you."

"About what?"

"They took time finding what flight you were on, I guess, because by the time they got through to us and we checked with the Port Authority out at JFK airport, you'd gone."

"Why would they want me in Honolulu?"

"The Port Authority told us you'd changed your plans, you'd booked into this hotel – so – I got here to meet you."

"That's all very thorough of you, Mr. Pagnucco, but why?"

"Well, Mr. Heysen, it's my duty now to warn you that you don't need to answer . . ."

"Yes, I know all that . . ."

"Okay. Mr. Heysen, it seems that Honolulu think you can help them with a homicide case."

"You're joking."

He shook his head. He had light brown hair and light brown eyes that were still and calm, the kind of unnerving calm that cops have, and it says to you: I have all the time in the world, sport, and for you it's running out.

"I don't know about any homicide," I told him.

"I don't know much about it myself, Mr. Heysen. I'm just talking to you because Honolulu asked us to find you. Can I have your passport and visa, please?"

I gave him my papers. He glanced at them, jotted their numbers down in his little black book, and handed them back.

"Why did you leave Honolulu, Mr. Heysen?"

"To come to New York."

"Why?"

"I'm a tourist."

"What were your movements the night before you left?"

"I went to a lanai party, my host was David Davidoff, a New Yorker. I got there around six p.m. I was there till around two a.m. then I left and walked back to my hotel. I checked out in the morning and flew here."

"Did you leave the party with anybody?"

"A few of us left in a group but we went our separate ways."

"Who left with you?"

"I wouldn't remember their names. They were strangers to me. Anyway, I was well tanked up."

"You'd been drinking?"

34

"It was a party."

"Sure, of course it was. What time did you get back to your hotel?"

"Ten or fifteen minutes after I left the party."

"Did you at any time during the night go to the Reef Hotel?"

"Which one is the Reef?"

"I've never been to Honolulu, Mr. Heysen."

"I was nowhere near any other hotel."

"How long will you be in New York?"

"A week, perhaps two."

"As long as it takes you to finish your business here?"

"I'm not here on business. I'm a tourist."

"Sure, of course you are. Will you be staying in this hotel the whole time?"

"What you're saying is, you don't want me to leave town without letting you know."

"That would make things easier for us. Honolulu might need to ask you for more help."

"I don't think so. But I'll let you know if I'm leaving."

"Thanks, Mr. Heysen. Did you meet Sandy Lee at the party or beforehand?"

"Who's he?"

"A she, Mr. Heysen. Honolulu girl."

"There were a lot of Honolulu girls at the party."

"Sounds a good party."

"It was alright."

"And you drank a lot?"

"Some. Mr. Pagnucco, who was Sandy Lee?"

"A girl called Sandy Lee was murdered at the Reef Hotel, Mr. Heysen. She was at the party with you . . ."

"Not with me she wasn't. I wouldn't know your Sandy Lee if she . . ."

"Okay, she was at the same party you were at. She was later found murdered."

I remained silent, thinking about it. I said, "I'm sorry I can't help you. She could have been any one of the girls at the party. It was a big party – it kind of spread itself out over a wide area. I'd like to help you – I told you, I work pretty close to the police back home."

"I'll be checking with the Sydney police when I get back to my office, Mr. Heysen."

Great stuff, I thought. Certainly I worked with them but they had no deep and abiding love for me.

"Strictly routine," he said, "we just have to check out any information, then we pass it back to Honolulu."

"I understand."

"It's an arrangement we have."

"Of course."

"Why didn't you go on to Rio?"

"I changed my mind."

"You wouldn't object to fingerprinting, Mr. Heysen?"

"Fingerprinting?"

"Honolulu went over the dead girl's room for prints and if your prints don't correspond . . ."

"Do Honolulu suspect me?"

"You might have a better idea about that than me, Mr. Heysen."

"I was nowhere near any dead girl's room. Why would they want my fingerprints?"

"It may help clear you."

"If I need any clearing, I'll let you know."

"Alright Mr. Heysen."

"The idea's ridiculous, naturally."

"I don't know anything about it, Mr. Heysen. I'm just asking the questions for Honolulu."

He picked up his coat. "You've been helpful, thanks a lot. If we need you, we'll contact you here – and you'll let us know if you're leaving?"

"Certainly. Glad to help."

I went to the door with him and he said, "Enjoy your visit to New York, Mr. Heysen. We call it Fun City, U.S.A. I hope you find it that way."

"Thanks Mr. Pagnucco."

And I closed the door after him.

Chapter 9

I kicked my shoes off. Sitting about in aircraft for hours plays hell with your feet. Sometimes it's as if you'd walked all the way.

I reached into my pocket for my own little black book. I sat by the phone and flipped through the pages to find Dave Angove's New York number.

At least I wasn't completely alone in the city. Laidlaw Press, my employer, that one-man empire of newspapers, radio and television stations, had a New York office, and the man here was Dave Angove. We had known each other since long ago when Dave was one of Laidlaw's editors and I was an all-night disc jockey on one of Laidlaw's radio stations. It was time we met again.

"Peter Heysen? Pete! Here in New York?"

"Almost on your doorstep, Dave."

"Good news," and then a pause and, "or is it bad news? What's your trouble, Pete?"

"Trouble, Dave?"

"I remember too many times, Pete. If you were here for pleasure, you'd have forewarned me – I'd have had a cable from Laidlaw telling me not to let you spend too much company money."

"Dave, where can we talk?"

"You've only just arrived?"

"Yeah."

"And you have that tone of voice already? You're in a hurry?"

"You might say that, Dave."

"I'm in the East Seventies."

"That means a hell of a lot to me."

"Okay, where are you calling from?"

I gave him the name of my hotel.

"Stay there, Pete. I have to come downtown to my office, I'll call by on the way."

"Thanks, Dave. I'll be in the bar."

"At this hour?"

"Sorry. I suppose you've still got the taste of cornflakes and

37

toothpaste in your mouth. I've been travelling so long it feels like the middle of tomorrow night."

"Alright, I'll meet you in the bar. Order me something sensible, a Bitter Lemon."

I waited for him in the brass and glitter hotel bar, slaking my travellers' thirst with a long beer then jolting my tired bones to life with a bourbon on the rocks, and then – not liking American beer much, and bourbon even less – I switched to scotch and stayed with it, thinking about a pretty girl called Sandy Lee and a clever cop called Pagnucco who was obviously doing it all by numbers but seemed to have guessed already how they added up. Perhaps I should have gone on to Rio anyhow, and stayed there forever.

"Peter Heysen."

I looked up, then stood and shook his hand.

"Hello, Dave."

"Slumped at the bar with your nose in a glass and your mind away somewhere on a private orgy of violence all your own."

"All this feature writing is going to your head, Dave."

He sat beside me, a slight little man with merry eyes. I ordered his Bitter Lemon.

We talked for five minutes about home and old friends of Dave's and about New York and his work here. His wife was here with him, missing her garden but enjoying pouring gold upon the heads of the New York clothiers.

"But about you," Dave finally said. "I was right when I said trouble?"

I looked at him and he grinned and said, "Yes, I thought it might be. Our favourite employer doesn't know you're here?"

"He thinks I'm wasting time lazing on the sun-warmed sands of Waikiki, when I should be preparing next year's show."

"You left Honolulu to come here at this time of year?"

"Honolulu was a little too hot for me."

"Let's hope you don't find Manhattan too cold. Tell me the story."

I looked at him again, slowly, and he understood. "Alright then, I know – I'll get the story when you're ready to give it. I'll rephrase the question. What can I do for you?"

"I'm looking for a woman, Dave. A very special one. She's the former wife of a man called Max Rolfe."

"That bastard?"

"You know him?" I asked.

"What newsman doesn't? International playboy is the category. A big player in the international set, but he stays out of the papers. Publicity shy. Stinks of money. Carries a Rothschild credit card. Unscrupulous if it suits him and it generally does, but he's odd in his way – has his own set of principles, I suppose."

"Like what?"

"He's uninhibited by any ethics in business! They say he pulled off a land deal in Mexico that left a lot of people homeless. Nasty stew about the whole thing. Politics, the works. Made his pile and walked away from it and a handful of Mexican politicians blew their careers. Then, so the story goes, he sank a fortune into rehabilitating flood victims in Peru. Still operates a big factory down there, at a loss so I hear, to provide work for the people."

"Guilt?"

"No, it's deeper than that. If you're with him he's with you, and he never seems to forget it even after any normal man would. I don't know what it was but somebody down in Peru must have done him a big favour once. Similar thing with his first wife."

"How many wives has he had?"

"Only two that anybody knows about. His first walked out on him, he treated her pretty hard if you can believe half what you hear in the trade. She sued for ridiculous alimony and got it, you know how it is in these American courts, and two years later she remarried so he stopped the payments. She didn't marry money, it must have been love, whoever he was. But it lasted only a few months and he was killed in a highway smash in California. What does Rolfe do? He's off the hook but he starts sending her the alimony cheques again."

"Why the hell?"

"He must have thought she needed it. It's what I said, if you're with him he doesn't forget you quickly."

"But with strangers he couldn't care less, is that right?"

"No, not exactly. If it's business he'll rob you of your wooden leg. Yet you hear stories of him pulling total strangers out of a hole just because he happens to be close by. What motivates him? A normally decent man with a highly overactive monkey gland, I suspect. And a strong sense of self-preservation."

39

"A strange one," I said. "What about his second wife?"

Dave finished his drink. "I have to get to the office," he said. "Walk along with me, I'll tell you about her."

We went out into the sharp, cold wind. This was a sensation I had to get accustomed to: far too much heat indoors anywhere and far too much cold outdoors everywhere.

Hands plunged into the pockets of my summer suit, I hurried along Madison Avenue with Dave. Passers by, cocooned in heavy coats, glanced at me suspiciously and hurried on.

"His second wife was Elizabeth," Dave said. "I don't know who she was or where she came from, but she was a gorgeous piece, blonde and slim and – you know how it is. An all-American girl, I believe, but the two of them must have made a striking pair with their tall Nordic looks. It seems they led a hectic life together but Rolfe wasn't always the most faithful husband you ever heard of. She left him and married John Cunningham, another millionaire of a different sort. An old man, he keeps mostly to himself."

"Sounds like she'd always land on her feet," I said.

"She gets around a lot without him. That's Saks over there and the Rockefeller Center across the way! We're on Fifth Avenue now. If you keep moving ahead you'll reach Central Park."

"Thanks, I'll just drop dead from the cold right here."

"You certainly arrived in a hurry."

"What's she like?" I asked Dave.

"Strictly cafe society. I suppose you'd call them disco society these days. Not the old inherited money group that lives out of town and comes in quietly. She's with the new money group who live in Manhattan penthouses and who like to be seen and written about."

"More easily approachable," I said.

He grinned. "Probably. A peculiar bird in her own way. Beautiful, cold, eccentric." He thought for a moment. "There are a few nightspots where you might bump into her if you can't arrange a smoother introduction."

"Can you?" I asked him.

"Doubtful."

"Then she'll have to be bumped into."

"I could find out more for you. If you look down through there you can see the Chrysler Building – back up that way is the Empire State, you'll have to go up to the top of it while you're here, it's on the agenda for all tourists."

"I'm not a tourist, Dave."

"From the 86th floor to the 102nd they don't number the floors on the elevator indicator, they give it in heights above sea level, the kind of American bulldust I admire."

"How do you find out more about her for me, Dave?"

"Take a walk down that way to Lexington Avenue sometime, you'll find the Grolier Building. An old building, looks gold-plated, the whole thing. Smog plays hell with the colour though, it mostly looks more like urine. But you've got to see it."

"Dave?"

"Okay. They have an evening sheet here, a new one with a triple-hyphen name, a good paper if it lasts. Does the name Suzy Knickerbocker mean anything to you?"

"Gossip? The rich and famous, that kind of thing?"

"Correct. The lady who writes it is a friend, in a way. We trade favours. I have a couple of ways into the expatriate British society in New York and she gets wind of some hard news from the U.N. crowd occasionally. We feed each other leads."

"You'll talk to Miss Knickers for me?"

"Sure. She won't set up anything for you but she'll tell me what she reasonably can about Elizabeth Cunningham's movements around town, then you'll be on your own. Down there is the Rockefeller Plaza and the outdoor ice-skating rink. Old ladies skating in mini-skirts. The finest and funniest free show in New York. My office is in the Center itself."

We entered the towering Rockefeller Center through the revolving doors and crossed the busy, high-ceilinged foyer to the elevators. Dave asked me, "What's important about Elizabeth Cunningham that you have to meet her?"

"It's like you and Miss Knickers," I said. "I think we can trade favours."

"I wouldn't mind trading one or two with her myself," he said. "It'd be big stakes if you're playing in that league."

Dave Angove's office was big and homely; heavy old furniture and deep leather armchairs, an impression of old, well-polished wood. There was a new electric typewriter on a stand by his desk. Outside in the main office there were a few empty desks littered with papers.

"I don't get the staff in Saturdays unless something breaks," Dave said. "The wire services carry all the meat anyway, we just worry about the gravy nine to five. I come in here Saturday mornings to do my column and get it off to Sydney by noon."

"When will you call Miss Knickers for me?"

He looked at his watch. "She's strictly night shift, she'll still be in bed if she's a sensible girl. Get the hotel to send your bill here, we're so far away from Laidlaw we can absorb it without much trouble. One of our away-from-home fringe benefits."

"Thanks, Dave. I'll leave you to work. I want to get some warm clothes. I'll have a look around the city and call you back later."

"If I'm not here, call me at home. I'll be there all weekend. You'll like it here Peter, if you give it time. When I first arrived in New York I took one look and grabbed a train for Washington. One look at Washington and I caught a plane back to New York."

"Dave, I'm sorry, all I want is a quiet vacation in Honolulu."

I spent an hour making further raids on my credit card account, buying a couple of winter suits and some sox and underwear and a warm topcoat. I wore the topcoat and had everything else delivered to my hotel.

I cashed a wad of travellers' cheques on the theory that I might need old-fashioned cash at any time and green bills are more negotiable no matter what they say at American Express.

I wandered around that small area of Manhattan between the Rockefeller Center and my hotel a few blocks away.

For a few moments I watched an old man on the ice in the Rockefeller Plaza, a black wool cap on his head and a permanent, distant, enigmatic smile on his face – dreaming, perhaps, of who knows what youthful and spirited orgies on the ice as he took every corner with one leg wiggling in front of him.

I looked at the girls and wished for bikinis and hot sun and noted how many of the girls chomped hungrily on chewing gum and I wondered if American men prefer a woman spearmint-flavoured rather than tasting like a woman.

Then I amused myself idly reading off the names of the cab companies as their bright yellow cabs butted their way through the traffic: there was *Cut* and *Acne* and *Bumper* and *Grin* and there was *Hunch* and *Speedway* and *Dyke* and the *Fanny Service Corp.* Odd that the word *fanny* has a whole new anatomical location inside the United States.

I also liked the man who provides the portable toilets for construction workers, *Jobsite Johnny, Inc,* and a baker called *Fink.*

This could be my last day on earth and here I was seeking mobile graffiti on street corners. I went back to my hotel for a quick lunch then up to my room to call Dave Angove.

"If you go up to Central Park right now," he said, "you'll spot Elizabeth Cunningham exercising her dogs – three of them, big German Shepherds."

"How does she keep dogs like that in an apartment?"

"You haven't seen her apartment. Pete, there's an entrance to Central Park on Fifth at Seventy-Second Street, go in there and start walking and you'll somewhere find a blonde with three dogs. That's Elizabeth Cunningham."

"Thanks Dave."

"One other thing."

"What's that?"

"I checked with another source. John Cunningham has a meat-packing business. He's seventy-odd by his own admission."

"With a young, blonde wife," I said.

"Maybe she's sapping all the old boy's strength," Dave said. "The Cunningham business has been going bad for some time and Cunningham himself is out on a limb, he stands to lose the lot. I don't know if that helps you."

"Thanks Dave."

I put a fresh white handkerchief in the jacket of my new suit and put on my new coat and I went down in the elevator. I had my shoes buffed to a high polish and I sucked in a deep breath of superheated hotel air and walked out into the cold.

I was a visitor to New York about to take a quiet stroll through Central Park, about to accidentally meet the former wife of a man who had saved one stranger from a heavy surf and thrown another towards the arms of the Honolulu Police Department.

Chapter 10

New York's Central Park is one of the last remaining moments of sanity in a half-mad city. The most valuable piece of undeveloped real estate in the world has been left inviolate and untouchable; the rest of the narrow rocky island of Manhattan may be a preposterous monument to the herd instinct but in Central Park there is a chance for a man or a woman to be alone. Without it, New York would be like living in a submarine.

I entered the park as Dave Angove had instructed me and crossed open ground then followed a path through trees, a path strewn with the last of the fallen leaves of autumn, and I came to a pond where a group of men watched by envious children sailed elaborate model boats, manipulating them with long poles.

I walked up and over a rise, past a lake where a few hardy ones were putting in some energetic rowing before the lake finally iced over, then suddenly I was alone, walking through a small forest and watching wild squirrels, dozens of them, rushing about gathering the last scraps of food before the winter that was already in the air. I wished I had time to buy a barrel of peanuts and sit and feed them and think about anything but the hot breath of the Honolulu Police Department.

I walked on slowly with the branches of the trees rattling leafless in the wind above my head. There was a grey, misty quality to the afternoon. And through the trees I could see the shape of an old castle.

I followed a narrow path and approached a courtyard with the castle beyond it, an old grey castle, not very big, small enough for a fairytale. And there, in a setting that suited her perfectly, I saw Elizabeth Cunningham for the first time: aloof, unmoving and beautiful with three big German Shepherd dogs standing at heel.

She couldn't be anybody else. She was tall with ash-blonde hair to her shoulders, and she wore knee-length black boots and a white fur coat with a high collar and a loose belt of the same fur.

She stood there stiffly against the backdrop of the old castle. She watched me as I neared her. Slowly, deliberately, she pointed to me from fifty yards away and I saw her speak to her dogs and suddenly they were up and coming at me.

They rushed me silently, not barking, not whimpering, just the tearing sounds of their feet and nails on the stone courtyard as they spread out and came at me, teeth bared.

I ran the last few steps up onto the courtyard to deny the dogs any advantage and I started to tug at my coat: I had some wild idea I might smother the first dog under my coat and deal with the others in some similarly professional and thoroughly unperturbed manner.

But I was saved from the heroics by Elizabeth Cunningham. She snapped out one sharp word and the dogs turned in a fluid movement and trotted back to her, wagging their tails.

I buttoned up my coat again and took a closer look at Mrs. Elizabeth Cunningham. She was clearly a lady with an exceptional sense of humour.

I walked towards her, slowly, my eyes on her but my mind on her dogs.

She began to smile. It was a warm smile but with perhaps a trace too much self-assurance. If a woman has just sooled three dogs onto you, no matter for what sport or joke, you'd like her to smile at you with at least a hint of apprehension. But the lovely Mrs. Cunningham was all cool.

"I hope they didn't frighten you," she said.

"They did."

"They usually do. I let them have a squirrel sometimes. It's good for their egos." Her smile changed imperceptibly and it suggested for a moment the spoilt brat. "Most people run away when they see the dogs coming. People are scared of German Shepherds, they think they get nasty in their old age and eat little children or something."

"All rubbish," I said. "They're really very placid animals if you treat them right. Do you make a habit of sooling them onto people?"

I stood ten feet away from her now, being appraised by her like a slave at auction.

"Oh," she said, "you're English, aren't you."

"Australian."

"That's a shame. I have a friend who's an Englishman. The dogs love him."

"I'm sorry to disappoint the dogs."

"Were you really going to fight them?"

"It's an old Australian custom."

"How charming." And having looked me over with her steady green eyes – and, presumably, having rejected me – she turned to stride away calmly with her dogs in tow.

"Don't go yet Mrs. Cunningham, I want to talk with you."

She paused and turned to look back at me. With the old castle background she was definitely somebody's fairytale princess, except that she had the eyes of a conniving witch. She stared at me, straight and hard.

"You're wondering," I began, "how I know your name . . ."

"Most people in New York know me."

"Most people? Or only the ones who matter?"

She cocked her head to one side. "My husband told me I shouldn't talk to newspapermen."

"Which husband?"

"That was hardly in good taste. Who are you, what do you want?"

"I want to talk with you about Max Rolfe."

Her expression of cool arrogance slipped for a moment and I caught a fleeting glimpse of angry emotion but it passed quickly. "You're a friend of Max's?"

"Hardly a friend."

"That's something we can say for you. What about him?"

"Isn't there a better place we can talk than in a public park?"

"Tell me about Max."

"I understand he wants to rescue you – that's what he told me, he's going to rescue you from your present husband. Is he out of his mind? I met him in Honolulu . . ."

"*Rescue* me?" She grinned. "He wants me back?"

"You know him better than I do, Mrs. Cunningham."

"I wonder about that. You say you met him in Honolulu. When?"

"Two days ago. He left yesterday for Rio de Janeiro."

She came closer to me now, her face more thoughtful, her green eyes trying to pry into my mind.

"Are you sure he left for Rio?"

"Certain," I said. I wasn't certain at all; with a man like Rolfe, nothing is ever certain, but with a woman like Elizabeth it helps to be positive.

Her eyes stayed intently on mine for a second longer while

she absorbed what I had told her. Then, "Who are you?"

"Peter Heysen. I came to New York to meet you."

"Then we'd better talk back at my apartment." She slipped her arm quickly through mine. "Do you like dogs, Mr. Heysen?"

"I don't know much about thoroughbreds."

She held my arm firmly. "I know a lot about thoroughbreds, Mr. Heysen. I've made a close study of thoroughbreds."

And the dogs followed us back through Central Park and across Fifth Avenue and up in an elevator that played soft music and into her apartment.

Chapter 11

The apartment had at least a dozen rooms, furnished to please a Medici. Statuary and tapestries, heavy drapes, scattered gilt-framed oils of men on horses. With the exception of the concealed lighting, an occasional piece of wildly modern sculpture, and the environment control dial by the door of every room, it was Hollywood Renaissance. But the props were real.

It seemed to me that the few small, incongruous pieces of modern sculpture may have been Elizabeth Cunningham's only contribution to the clutter, and it also seemed that she was as out of place here as I was.

The dogs ran obediently onto a terrace entirely enclosed by glass, a huge fifteenth floor all-glass kennel with a view of Central Park and all-year temperature control.

John Cunningham, when he bought this place, had obviously taken two large apartments one above the other, punched a hole in the floor of the higher one, then connected the two with a wide spiral staircase. I hoped I might meet John Cunningham one day.

She took my coat and tossed it over an antique settee in the entrance foyer and then, after she had closed the door on her dogs, she led me quickly into a small sitting-room off the main living room; this smaller room was as coldly museum-like as the rest of the apartment, the walls encrusted with miniature paintings, but somebody had attempted to make it more feminine with fresh pastel colours and a few frills and flounces on the curtains and upholstery.

She waved me to sit with her on the sofa, and a set of six bone china demitasse coffee cups waited for us on a coffee table.

We had only just sat down and the door opened again. It was Elizabeth Cunningham's maid, with coffee, and already the scenery began to improve.

She wore a light blue uniform, simply cut but cut to fit where it should. She too was a blonde but there was a honey glow in her hair and warmth in her eyes, and a naturally fluid poise in all her movements. All of her moved together at the same time as she crossed the room towards us with the coffee on a silver tray.

"Ah, Helga, this is Mr. Heysen."

I stood up and we said hello and I was vaguely aware of my hostess dismissing her briefly with a tiny wave of her hand, but our eyes met for an instant of promises probably never destined to be fulfilled. She smiled quickly, put the coffee on the table, then glanced up again and turned and left the room.

I sat down, watching Helga's round bottom depart through the door, pondering aimlessly on how it is that the backs of some young ladies' knees can be so disturbing. The things that can turn a man on.

"Pretty, isn't she?" Elizabeth said.

"I'll bet she brews good coffee."

"Yes. Sugar and cream?"

"Just sugar."

"It's a shame about Helga. Sweet girl. But she has her problems. She has few boy friends and can't keep those she does get."

I looked back at the door through which Helga had departed. "Are you sure about that?"

"I always know what's going on around me. She tried changing her deodorant but it goes deeper than that."

"I'll bet you're very nice to her."

But having successfully destroyed Helga's character, Elizabeth Cunningham had already put her maid out of her thoughts.

"Two sugars?" she asked.

"One, thanks Elizabeth." We had settled easily into a first-name relationship on our walk across the park.

She gave me my coffee and I balanced it awkwardly on my knee. The demitasse was designed in days too delicate for me; each contains no more than a mouthful and I put it back on the table to gloat over a while before I drank it.

"Now," Elizabeth said, "about Max."

"Sitting here in your apartment in New York," I said, "it sounds silly but in Honolulu it didn't seem so silly. It was the way he talked. He meant it. He wants to get you away from your present husband."

"Why would he want to do that? Max wouldn't want me around his neck again, why would he want to take me away from a perfect old dear like John Cunningham?"

"I can only tell you what he told me. He said it was for your sake . . ."

"My sake! Since when did Max Rolfe do anything for my sake?"

"He said you were too good for your present husband – you deserved a better life, a more exciting life – he didn't seem to think your perfect old dear was much good for you. It would take an unusual man to think that way."

"He *is* unusual. But you're making this up."

"Sorry, that's how I got it from him. Davidoff agreed, he told me . . ."

"David Davidoff?"

"Yes."

"David was in Honolulu?"

"He had a party . . ."

"And Max was there? Oh yes, I can picture that. Max seduced some poor little island girl. . . ."

I glanced at her and she caught my look and laughed. "What else would Max do?" she asked. "He was my husband, I know him too well."

"Obviously."

"So he really does want to protect me from the awful clutches of poor John? Even David Davidoff thinks so." She sipped her coffee. "Really, I guess, it's the kind of silly idea that would get into Max's head. He told me once that it wasn't so much the fact that I was unfaithful, it was the people I chose to be unfaithful *with* that shook him. Isn't that silly?"

"Of course."

"I mean, it's my body, I can do whatever I like with it."

"Clearly."

She looked at me quickly and grinned and then she looked away and asked, casually, "Why are you here telling me all this, Peter?"

"I was coming to New York anyway – I was on my way here and I thought, Elizabeth Cunningham is a lady who should be tipped off."

"It's not that simple, is it, Peter? Are you trying to get back at Max for something he did to you, is that it?"

"You might put it that way." It was a lame excuse and I knew it – and she knew it too – but I could think of no better one, and there was no way I was going to tell her yet my real reason for contacting her. She was plainly the kind of woman who would use me if she could, and I was bent on using her if I could, which not only made us a particularly charming pair but also dimmed the likelihood of any shared confidences, at least at this stage of the play.

"You're not telling me the truth, Peter."

"Elizabeth, your former husband is a con-man. You know it, I'm sure. He took out round one against me. If I can give you fair warning of what Max has in mind for you, if I can foul his little game in some small way, perhaps that puts me slightly ahead in round two."

"Seriously Peter . . ." and the gentle amusement in her eyes slowly cooled, "where's the benefit in this for you?"

"You could tell me where I might find Max."

"You said he went to Rio."

"Perhaps he did. And then again, maybe he came to New York to see you."

"He hasn't called me. And if he's here I wouldn't know where he'd stay. What did he do to you, did something happen in Honolulu . . . something you have to square off with him?"

"You might put it like that."

"What was it? If you want me to help, I want to know why."

"That's between Max and myself."

She stood up and smoothed down the skirt of her loose-waisted dress. She reached for the zippers of her soft black boots and slipped her slender legs out of them.

"Peter, I can't help you much if you won't tell me what it's all about. And you wouldn't be here if you didn't want my help."

"You have nice legs."

"Did Max tell you that?"

"He didn't talk about you that way."

"He didn't?" She seemed surprised. "Now that *is* unusual. He always used to tell other people what I was like, especially he told other men. Max got drunk with you in Honolulu and he told you some great stories about his ex-wife, the ex-girl-about-town, right?"

"No he didn't." Her lines were coming from an old script and I could sense trouble.

"Peter, I want to know what happened in Honolulu. I'll help you any way you like with Max, if you'll tell me about Honolulu."

"That's not why I came here, Elizabeth."

She put her hands high behind her neck and unhooked the top of her dress. She loosened the zipper right down her back.

She said, "Is that why you came here?"

Her dress fell forward off one shoulder and her bra was about as transparent as her intentions. I picked up the demitasse and drained it and all but sank my teeth into the bone china.

I told her, "I wish you'd put your clothes on or have a cold shower or something. I asked you where I can find Max. If you can't help me that's too bad. I don't want to talk about Honolulu."

She stared back at me and pursed her lips, thinking about me – and I was having trouble understanding myself why I didn't leap upon her making crude animal noises in my throat – and then, quickly, she did up her dress.

I stood and awkwardly crossed the room away from her to the window and I looked down into Central Park. The trees in the park were thin pencil lines through the afternoon mist. In a playground below, a group of silent unmoving Negro women in heavy old topcoats watched a hectic tribe of little white children in quilted parkas.

"New York," I said, "is a very sophisticated town, isn't it, Mrs. Cunningham."

Chapter 12

I turned and she was fully clothed, boots and all, and perched on the sofa.

I said, "It would have been a nice bonus under different circumstances. But all I want is to find Max Rolfe."

"And I want to know what happened in Honolulu." It was a small voice now, young, almost pleading. "I don't know where he is – but if he turns up I'll tell you, if you'll tell me about Honolulu."

"What happened in Honolulu wouldn't make any difference to you."

She shook her head. "I wish I could be sure of that. Where are you staying in New York?"

I told her my hotel.

"Will you have dinner here, with me and my husband?"

I had to smile. "You know, this *is* a sophisticated town."

She raised her head and I looked into her eyes for the first time since she had taken off her boots. I asked her, "Why did you do it, Elizabeth?"

"I have to know."

"Kind of a drastic way to find out, wasn't it?"

"I can be a drastic woman when it suits."

"No kidding?"

She stood up now and approached me. She seemed softer now, more subdued. "The thought of Max Rolfe coming here frightens me – he's a ruthless man, Peter. He wouldn't just want to take me away from John. If that's what he said, then you can be sure he wants more than that. Maybe what happened in Honolulu between you two has something to do with it. He swore once that he'd ruin me completely."

"Could he?"

"Anything is possible for Max Rolfe." She ran her hands through her hair. "I'm sorry if I upset you – that was a pretty mean tactic, wasn't it?"

"Let's say it was a little hard."

"Rolfe," she said and it was almost as if she said it to herself. "I've seen him do things to people – just for the sake of doing them."

She shook her head as if to throw off the thought and she laughed. "Thank God I got away from him when I did. Look – will you stay for a drink? I promise, no monkey business. You say this is round two between you and Max. Well I don't know what it's all about and you're sure not going to tell me, but maybe I can tell you a little about him. I guess I'm more on your side than I am on his."

I thought about it. I was uncertain.

"Spit on my finger," she said lightly, "and cross my heart. I'll sit right across the room from you and we'll just talk."

I tried to read her expression. It was steady, relaxed.

"Okay," I told her, "I could use a drink."

She chuckled. "I expect you could."

She talked easily about Max Rolfe for half an hour and told me little that I didn't know. She let me mix the martinis. I don't know how many I mixed. She sat facing me for a while then she joined me on the sofa to show me some old photographs. Daylight faded and she switched on a small wall lamp that gave off a soft glow like vintage red wine. She pushed the old shots aside and removed her boots and we talked lazily about Honolulu, places we had been and places we would like to go.

I was tired from the fears of the past twenty-four hours, and the martinis were strong, and I was born a fool over women.

"Max Rolfe set me up for murder," I said.

We lay now on the sofa and she had full control of the situation, taking me through a rare kind of love-making, smiling all the while.

I said, "Rolfe got out of Honolulu before they could find anything on him. I doubt if they ever will."

I told her how he passed the buck to me, how I would be as much under suspicion as Rolfe, if they could get any evidence at all on us, which was likely.

I was drunk on more than martinis. I stumbled out of her apartment into the sudden blast of bitter night cold on Fifth Avenue. I knew I had told her everything about Honolulu, every little detail, and she had said nothing at all.

How dumb, how stupid, can a man get? How sensual can a woman get?

Chapter 13

I walked the mile or so along Madison Avenue back to my hotel with the cold wind on my back, peering in at some of the mad little galleries along that part of the city. Enough to sober anybody.

A sign in a bank offered free to its Christmas Savings Club members a combination flashlight, key ring and emergency police whistle. I sobered some more.

There is a happy anonymity about walking in the dark on a cold night; people rush by, not seeing you through their streaming eyes, caring only for the warmth of their apartments. Nobody looks at you, nobody wants to bother you. And as my ears grew numb, my thick-witted mind became sharper, and my anger with myself increased.

Elizabeth Cunningham had pulled out all the stops to discover what I knew about Max Rolfe in Honolulu. She hadn't seemed surprised, she had in fact seemed only drowsily interested, yet she had asked too many pertinent questions for me to feel comfortable now. I had gone to her to find out more about Max Rolfe and had come away empty-handed, leaving her knowing as much about that Honolulu night as I knew. I had the disquieting feeling that she may know a good deal more about the night.

The possibility wasn't new to me but I brought it out and examined it again: if Rolfe had, as he claimed, not killed the girl in the hotel, then some other person had done it to incriminate Rolfe. Somebody wanted Rolfe in trouble. Somebody wanted him alive but out of the way. Perhaps Rolfe had known it all along and had set me up quickly. It made some kind of sense: I could see no other reason why Rolfe would make sure I stayed close to him to catch the ball when he bounced it. Plainly, if that much were true, he had felt that a man with his own crime show on television would be an ideal person to take the ball for him. How wrong he could be.

The next question followed logically: if Rolfe set *me* up, who set *him* up? He was a man with a world full of enemies. Elizabeth Cunningham was possibly the least of them. But it was a thought to cling to and I clung to it back to my hotel.

The warmth of the hotel foyer made my face tingle as I came in off the cold street. I removed my coat and crossed to the desk for my key and then I spotted Pagnucco sitting patiently waiting for me.

He nodded when he knew I had seen him and he stood up slowly and came towards me.

"Kind of cold out there after Honolulu," he said.

I asked him, "Do you want to talk to me here or in my room?"

"It's maybe just a little too public down here, Mr. Heysen."

He followed me while I got my key, and with the key there was a message from the hotel operator: *Mr. Angove called. Mr. Pagnucco was asking him about you. Mr. Angove told him nothing you wouldn't. Please call Mr. Angove.* I thanked the desk clerk and went to screw up the paper but I saw Pagnucco looking at it. He would get a copy from the operator anyway so I passed it to him.

Pagnucco glanced at it. "Mr. Angove sure is a friend of yours." He grinned gently. "He's right, he didn't tell me anything you wouldn't."

"What did you ask him?"

"I asked him if he knew what you were doing in the Reef Hotel all night."

"You'd better come up to my room," I said.

I called room service for a bottle of scotch and some ice and I sprawled weakly on the bed. Detective Frank Pagnucco of the D.A.'s office sat in a chair and watched me.

I asked him, "How did Honolulu know I was at the Reef?"

"They traced Sandy Lee, the dead girl, to a lanai party..."

"Davidoff's party," I said.

"Right. Honolulu knew you were there, that part of your story checks. They had a photograph of you..."

"From the tourist press," I said.

"I wouldn't know where they got the shot. But they canvassed the guests at the hotel and a carload of people in the hotel carpark recognised you, said you were one of a group who came in stoned off the beach and got into an elevator." He glanced at his notebook. "You, two island girls, and a blond man. Let's say one of the girls was Sandy Lee. Who was the blond man and what was the other girl's name?"

"No idea."

"Heysen, it would be easier for you in the long haul if you . . ."

"Pagnucco, it never happened. Not the way you say. I wasn't even there, I was nowhere near any other hotel. How come they showed only *my* picture to the hotel guests, why just me?"

"Sandy Lee was last seen alive at the Davidoff party. You were seen leaving with her."

"Me, *with* her?"

"She was in your group of four who left the Davidoff party late. Honolulu did a quick check and found a shot of you. I guess you could be right, they may have found the shot in press files. That's routine anyplace if you want a shot of a guy. So they hawked the shot around the Reef Hotel because that's where Sandy Lee was found."

"And now they think I went into the hotel with her and two others."

"They know it. They also know you came out again well after daybreak. The desk clerk remembered you. You were in the hotel all night."

"It looks bad for me."

"It does."

The scotch came on a tray and I signed for it and closed the door. "Does the condemned man get a drink before you arrest him?" I asked.

Pagnucco smiled for the second time this night. He scratched his head. He eyed the bottle so I put ice in two glasses. "To tell you the honest truth," he said, "nobody said I should arrest you."

"You're joking. I went into the hotel with the girl and I was there all night. I must have killed her. I'm guilty. Do they have capital punishment in Hawaii?"

He stared at the ceiling. "They used the noose there for a long time, just like the British. It'd be kind of homely for you. But they haven't hanged a man in a long time." He looked at me slowly. "Do you deny you were in the Reef Hotel?"

"Of course I do. I left the Davidoff party and went home direct. A couple of drunks in a gloomy carpark thought they saw me. A sleepy desk clerk thought he saw me . . ."

"You deny it, right?"

"That's what I'm saying to you."

"I'm asking the questions, that's all." He thanked me for

the scotch I handed him. "There is just one small thing – I have to ask you for your passport."

I found it and gave it to him. It was like parting with a large fragment of my freedom. He put it deep into his breast pocket and raised his glass to me and we both drank. I drank more deeply than he did and I refilled my glass immediately.

"Well," I said, "that about puts the seal on it, doesn't it? Do you want my prints now?"

He shook his head. "Honolulu got them from your own hotel room."

"Naturally, why didn't I think of that?"

"Is there anything else you'd like to tell me, Mr. Heysen, before I notify Honolulu?"

"No thanks. I'll just sit here and finish the bottle."

"You won't do anything . . ."

"Anything foolish? I've worked with the police for a long time, Mr. Pagnucco."

"Sure you have. Thanks for the drink, Mr. Heysen."

"Okay. And thanks for the tip."

"Tip, Mr. Heysen?"

"Yes. I'm pretty much in the clear. And you know it."

"How's that?"

"They've got some witnesses who saw me all over Honolulu but they don't want to take me in. They've got my prints but they still don't want me. Mr. Pagnucco, you know what that means."

He stood up and reached for his coat. I got off the bed to open the door for him. "It means," I said, "that in Honolulu they know the evidence of a couple of drunks and a sleepy desk clerk just isn't enough to hold a man."

"And the prints, Mr. Heysen?"

"If they've got my prints and still don't want me, it means they didn't find a trace of my prints in the dead girl's room. If they *had* found my prints anywhere near that room I'd be chained to your wrist by now and halfway to Honolulu."

And Pagnucco smiled for the third time that night. "Mr. Heysen, you certainly have worked with the police before, no doubt about that." And there the smile left him. "So you won't mind if I tell you what else it means. It means they have some kind of a lead pointing right at you. And I'm sure you know, Mr. Heysen, that when a cop finds one tiny little piece of evidence he works around it and works around it some more until he gets what he needs. It takes time but it nearly always works – all you want is a few witnesses and a desk clerk to point you in the right direction." He patted his breastpocket. "Meantime, you'll get a receipt for your passport. Goodnight, Mr. Heysen."

I didn't say anything. I watched him go and I closed the door softly and walked slowly back to the whisky bottle.

I poured a drink and called Dave Angove. I told him about my passport but not much more. The less he knew right now, the better. There was no future for either of us in involving Dave. He promised me help when I needed it and I promised him a story if I ever had one. But we both knew just how much help he could give me if the Honolulu Police Department blew the whistle on me. Perhaps his wife could send me a fruit cake in jail.

Chapter 14

I awoke with the knowledge that last night I had worried my way through a bottle of scotch, I had slept deeply after it, and that it was now a crisp Sunday morning in New York and I was a free man. It could be my last free day for a long time.

I hurried through breakfast and went out to see a little of New York. The sun was shining and it took some of the edge off the winter cold.

I left the downtown area of long, tall, shaded canyons then I walked and cabbed about in a search for my bearings.

When I had arrived in the city I had been gently lowered, it seemed, into the bowels of the city.

But now, from down here, it seemed as if the city had been lowered down upon its people. They had been swallowed whole by a cranky beast with clogged veins and its head in a cloud of soot.

Of all the big cities, London and Paris and Rome inspire affection almost immediately, Tokyo needs a bonfire and a whole new start, but New York, more than any of them, forces itself upon you demanding instant attention. It moves in fast with noise and spectacle and sheer size. It shouldn't have surprised me that New Yorkers seemed an especially tough breed; it would take a certain crusty exterior on a man to keep a city of such determined immensity at arm's length.

But it was as if the proportions of the city in all things were a deliberate ruse to hide itself, for it gradually softened and grew smaller with familiarity on that first day.

Like learning to understand another's accent, the sounds of New York began to belong there. The chaotic yet comparatively silent traffic of Paris seems right for a gracefully cluttered city. The richly noisy traffic of New York was equally right for the city. Every driver appeared to edge along through the cramped streets with one hand on his horn and the other on a St. Christopher medal. Somewhere I'd heard the New York story that the shortest time known to mankind is that infinitesimal fraction between the lights turning green and the guy who starts tooting half a block back, and now I was ready to believe it.

Overhead, helicopters clattered and jet planes whooped and on the streets the sirens screamed and howled all day from everywhere, adding spice to the staple crash and roar of the cars. The two-tone yodeling sirens were the most effective, burrowing down through the middle ear into the central nervous system, probably forcing confessions from reluctant police witnesses at a distance of five blocks.

And it had to mean something that the traffic on the busiest corners could not be trusted to traffic lights alone: it needed lights, a cop's hand signal to interpret them, his whistle to enforce them, and the occasional shout of direct encouragement, to keep the cars moving.

In the area where the buildings were biggest, the noise was greatest. Here, men tore at the gut of the city, tumbling great buildings to the ground and hauling them away as fill for a swamp or foundations for a new highway: the graveyards of the skyscrapers. And in their place other buildings were being stacked up before the old ones could be mourned, and all it took to do all this was noise; shattering, blasting, hammering noise. Obviously the resident population is stone deaf and has been lip-reading all these years without being aware of it.

I wasn't ready for how old it all seemed: street after street of old brownstone buildings rising no more than a few floors with iron fire escapes draped across their facades like fading matrons displaying their underwear. Necessity in the shape of an old city ordinance had put them there to save lives and necessity had, once again, found an accidental new art form. One day, when all the elaborate and fussy iron lace of New Orleans and Montparnasse and Woolloomooloo has been taken indoors to the museums, a street of New York fire escapes will be recognised as a thing of strange beauty.

The city store windows groped for new delights to attract the jaded customer: electric drills silver-plated and engraved all over by hand like the tattooed lady, gold-plated adjustable shower roses, artificial flowers made of mink, Lifesavers flavoured with root beer and instant daiquiri mix in powder form. Perhaps you could dust it on your underarms after a heavy night.

I rediscovered the American penchant for big words: a tap becomes a faucet, a lift becomes an elevator, a car becomes an automobile, a bus company that would carry no less passengers as Bus Inc., had become the Manhattan and Bronx Surface Transit Operating Authority, and the fancier drug stores – 'drug store', after all, is an intelligent and reasonable name for a store that dispenses drugs – had become chemists, pharmacies and apothecaries.

I sampled their buses with the endless name: fat American suspension and hard fibreglass seats. And progressively less seats and more standing room in each more recent design. One day very soon they will calculate that there are in every one hundred passengers two pregnant women, one cripple and one ancient lady, and they will provide only four seats for every ninety-six who must stand. They may even hand out free deodorant.

The Christmas decorations were coming out. Men were erecting exotic gilt fibre-glass shapes in flowing forms more than twice life size, representing the troubadors of less affluent times; immense neon trees were being set up across the high fronts of department stores, and a towering aluminium building had coloured baubles and asterisks hanging from it. Down the wide stretch of Park Avenue the traditional trees were being set up every few blocks.

I wished I could snatch hold of the feel of festivity. All I could sense was desperation and frustration at being here without a passport and with little chance of escaping, when I should be getting burnt in the Honolulu sun.

Elizabeth Cunningham was too much on my mind for me to see more of the city. I telephoned her from a public call box and her maid, Helga, answered.

"I'm sorry Mr. Heysen, Mr. and Mrs. Cunningham will be out of town until later this afternoon."

"Oh."

"Did you get their message?"

"Message?"

"Mrs. Cunningham asked me to call you at your hotel. You were not there so I left a message with the desk."

"I haven't been back."

"Mrs. Cunningham would like you to join her and Mr. Cunningham for dinner tonight at their home."

"Tonight?"

"Mrs. Cunningham apologises for such a late . . ."

"That's okay. Mr. Cunningham will be there as well, huh?"

"Yes." She paused and I could all but see her smiling. "Mr. Cunningham will be here all night, Mr. Heysen."

"Helga . . . it is Helga, isn't it? . . . you better tell Mrs. Cunningham I'm sorry, I just can't make it tonight. I'm sure she'll understand."

"I am sure she will, Mr. Heysen." Again the faintest trace of a smile in her voice. And the beginnings of an idea in the dirty depths of my mind.

"Helga, you didn't by any chance find my cigarette lighter about the place this morning, did you?"

"In which room, Mr. Heysen?"

I wondered if Elizabeth Cunningham's maid was always that subtle. I said, "In the – ah – look, perhaps I'd better call around, I think I know where I put it. I'm close by, maybe I could call in right away?"

"I am the only one here, Mr. Heysen. Mr. and Mrs. Cunningham are . . ."

"Out of town. I'll be right there."

I put the phone down. If this was my last day of freedom it might as well be fruitfully spent; the least I could do for myself was to test the loyalty – and the inside knowledge – of the one person who must know most about Elizabeth Cunningham's private life.

The moment she opened the door to the apartment I recalled the look that had passed between us so briefly when we last met; a look that had been only slightly felt and never recognised by either of us. It was there again. There was nothing immediately physical or sensual about it, simply a sensation of seeming to know each other, as if we already understood each other.

"Please come in, Mr. Heysen."

"Thank you, Helga."

She took my coat and folded it carefully over the arm of the settee where Elizabeth had so casually tossed it about this time yesterday.

"I looked in the most likely places," she was saying, "but no sign of your cigarette lighter. What kind was it?"

"Mostly I use book matches," I said.

"I think perhaps you had better come in here, Mr. Heysen."

I followed her through the now almost familiar main living room into the now too familiar little room where Elizabeth and I had spent so much of the day. And as I entered the room and saw the miniatures on the walls and the long sofa, I felt the strong physical presence of Elizabeth Cunningham, I felt again the sensations that were now almost twenty-four hours old.

We sat facing each other across the low coffee table and I began to feel uncomfortable, her gaze was too direct, too honest. I offered her a cigarette. She took it and then, with the sweetest of all possible smiles, offered me a light from an ornate silver table lighter. I had to smile with her.

She said, "I think . . . I think you did not lose your lighter at all. It is also clear to me you did not come here to see Mrs. Cunningham – or Mr. Cunningham. You are not about to hit me on the head and steal the Cunningham flatware. So, I think . . . you came to see me."

"Yes, I did, Helga."

"Why?"

"Firstly – ah – my name is Peter, please call me Peter. Secondly, why did I come? Well, I thought perhaps – ah – you might be able to help me."

"I know what you thought, Mr. Heysen."

"Peter."

"You thought I would tell you more about Mrs. Cunningham. It had to be that. You did not come here because of me. After one heavy afternoon with Elizabeth Cunningham you find it hard to look at another woman. It is usually that way, Mr. Heysen. My employer is what I think you call a good woman in bed, so I am to believe. And now with bribery or flattery or with some other way you will hope to learn more about her because there is something about her you cannot understand."

"Ouch. This has happened before, huh?"

"The last man tried to bribe me."

"And I'll bet you turned him down."

"Yes."

"Oh boy. Give me a lead, Helga – how do I open negotiations with you?"

"You tell me what you want to know."

"Why didn't I think of that? Okay. In brief, I'm in trouble – not a lot of trouble, just enough to make life uncomfortable. I thought Mrs. Cunningham might be able to help me but now I think she may even have something to do with it. I don't know what to think. Our meeting yesterday didn't go exactly as I'd planned, any more than this one is."

"She does have her way of changing the subject, doesn't she?"

"I take it you don't like her much?"

"What makes you say that, Mr. Heysen?"

"You'd have thrown me out long ago. But you can see something in this for you. You're nobody's dizzy blonde maid. You're working for the Cunninghams for a reason of your own and you're sitting here talking with me for a reason of your own, you're that kind of person."

She looked away from me then and slowly she nodded her head, absorbing what I had said.

"Mr. Heysen . . ."

"Peter."

"Perhaps we can–what do they say?–scratch each other's back?"

I eased myself more comfortably into the sofa, I relaxed a little more. "My back's pretty itchy right now. How about yours?"

She looked at the watch on her wrist. "We have two hours maybe. I will get some coffee and we can talk."

Chapter 15

The coffee came in big kitchen cups. I liked her even more.

"My real name," she said, "is Helga Koehler. But that sounds very strange now, even to my ears. I have been known as Helga Brandt for too long. It is a made-up name. Even Mr. Cunningham, I think, only knows me as Helga Brandt. So Helga Brandt I am.

"I came to the United States – oh, ten years, maybe eleven years ago, and then I was Helga Koehler, coming to U.C.L.A. to study for two years. I wanted to be a fabric designer, I wanted to work with one of the big German textile companies in Frankfurt. I had it all figured out. I would go to them and say, here, I have studied in America and you are looking for American export markets and I am a designer who has studied there, I know what the American people want." She shook her head. "It was all very simple."

"What went wrong, Helga?"

"I killed my teacher."

"You did what?"

She shrugged. "That also was very simple. I was pregnant by him and I killed him."

"Now, whoa! Come back six paces!"

She laughed. "I am sorry. I try not to think about it. Really, it was all very silly. I am from a very strict family. My parents are many years dead, they died when I was very young, but all my family were strict and they brought me up to believe in right and wrong. I am not so strict now. I have lived with Elizabeth Cunningham for almost ten years.

"His name was Bonifacio, Robert Bonifacio. He was very warm, much older than me, I thought he was handsome and with much talent – and I was a long way from all the aunts and the uncles. I got pregnant. My glamorous Italian-American lover thought it the funniest thing. He made jokes about it, that was how much he cared. And he could not marry me even if he wanted to, which he did not."

"He was already married?"

"What else? His wife Elizabeth would not let him go."

"Elizabeth?"

"The lady who gave you so much pleasure here in this room and later in the bedroom and again in this room."

"You must've been keeping tabs."

"I work here. And I know my employer."

"So you just up and killed Bonifacio?"

"We had an argument. No – we had many arguments. Do you know, he still wanted me? How do you like that? And one night in his home, after I had been in Elizabeth Bonifacio's bed trying to persuade my handsome lover he should do something to help me, we stood on the terrace and we argued and we argued. He laughed and he said I should jump over. Do you know, I nearly did?

"I climbed out onto the edge of the terrace. It was dark. The street was only six floors down. Not so far, but it frightened him and he knew I meant it. I do not think he cared, he just did not want me leaping off *his* terrace. He reached out to try and stop me and I grabbed him and he tried to pull me back onto the terrace."

"And in pulling you up, he fell down, right?"

"Or did I pull him down, Peter? I do not know. It all happened. I wanted him dead. But does that mean I wanted to kill him? They are two different things. But he was dead when they got to him."

"What happened to you?"

"Elizabeth Bonifacio was very kind to me, do you know that? She was *so* kind. The moment he fell she was there on the terrace with me . . ."

"She was in the apartment all the time?"

"Spying on us. She wanted divorce evidence. But this was better."

"Insurance?"

Helga nodded. "Elizabeth Bonifacio got me quickly out of the apartment and as far as the police knew I was nowhere near the place when it happened. They never even knew I had anything to do with Robert Bonifacio."

"Why did she do that for you?"

"His insurance policy paid twice for a death by accident. But Elizabeth Bonifacio was afraid they would not call it an accident if it was homicide."

"If it was homicide."

"It could have been, Peter. How do we know ? Sitting here now, I tell you I do not know if I killed him or even if he was trying to kill me. It was an argument. Who knows what you do in an argument like that ?"

"So Elizabeth Bonifacio collected double the money. Her husband fell off the terrace unaided and she collected. Why did she keep you with her ?"

"Suppose, Peter, I said to myself – the police have to know and the court has to decide did I kill a man or did he kill himself by persuading me out onto the edge of the terrace ?"

"Yes – then you'd have to give them all the facts."

"Of course. If I could not live with myself – and for a long time I could not, I had to stay with her because she was the only one who knew, the only one who would help – but if I could not live with myself then I would go to the police. Remember I was a young German girl, very strict but suddenly not so strict."

"And if you had gone to the law, Elizabeth would have been an accessory to swindling an insurance company."

"You see ? She had to keep me with her. She is not so sure of me even now, she must keep me close where she can watch me. She talked to me a lot about it in those days, she made it easier for me. At least I do not have the dreams about it any more. She helped me get rid of the baby, she took me to one of the best doctors in these things, right here in New York City."

"You both moved to New York ?"

"Here she was a beautiful woman from California, wealthy enough to have her own maid. It did not take her long. Five months after she got the insurance money and came East, she married Max Rolfe."

"And you still stayed with her."

"Whenever they were in the United States. I never moved outside the United States."

"You never went home to Germany ?"

"I write sometimes to my uncle. He is the only one left now and he is too old to care much. He knows I changed my name. He thinks it is because the Americans find it easier to say Brandt than Koehler."

"Why don't you just walk out ?"

"I came here as a German student called Helga Koehler. I had a student visa. It – expired. The immigration people never found Helga Koehler. Nobody ever traced me to Boni-facio. Who would ever connect the maid of the wealthy Mrs. Rolfe with a quiet student called Koehler. This country is too big."

"So you have no papers?"

"No papers, no name, no home. After ten years here I have to think hard if I want to speak German. Even if I wanted to go back to Germany, how could I leave without papers, with-out answering questions? I am tied to Elizabeth Cunningham and she is tied to me. And we are such good friends."

"I can just imagine it." I lit cigarettes for us. "But Helga..."

"Why do I tell you all that?"

"Yes."

"Because now we are equal. You know that I might be a killer and I know that you might be a killer."

"You what?"

"We both have our problems, yes? And both our problems have one thing together – Elizabeth Cunningham. If I killed Bonifacio, that has something to do with her. If you killed that poor girl in Honolulu, that also has something to do with my employer."

"How do you know...?"

"I think I will get some more coffee, then we can go on talking."

"You do that, Helga. You make it black and very strong."

Chapter 16

"What gives you the idea I killed a girl in Honolulu?"

"Did you kill her, Peter?"

"I didn't, but that's beside the point. How did you know about it?"

"I heard you with Elizabeth Cunningham."

"You really were keeping tabs, weren't you?"

"I did not hear all of it. I would not want to know all of it. But sometimes we do things because we want to know things, because it is necessary. You see, it is necessary for me to get away from Elizabeth Cunningham."

"So you heard my story."

"I heard you wanting to know about Max Rolfe. And I heard her persuading you to tell all about Honolulu, what happened there. You were not going to tell her, but she has her ways, mm?"

"She certainly does."

"She is very good, Peter?"

I drank some of my coffee. "Persuasive."

"You know all of this now – would you go back to bed with her if she offered?"

"Has that got anything to do with you, Helga?"

"No. I am too inquisitive. It is not so good for me. I have lived too long with this woman. I should not have asked you that."

"Tell me, Helga, does she ruin everything she touches?"

"Yes. Mr. Rolfe was a good man. Not always, but nearly always a good man. I had a thing for him, do you know what I mean? I think if he had wanted . . . but he was very conceited. And of course she played on that. She liked to hurt his conceit. It was a bad time she gave him. But still I think he loved her because she had – what is it? – the sort of energy that he has. Ambition, maybe. It makes her cruel sometimes but he liked that in her."

"Does he still love her, Helga?"

"How do I know? We have not seen him for a long time. But I think perhaps he does. I heard you tell her that he wants to get her away from Mr. Cunningham. Maybe he loves her?"

"Helga – do you think he could have killed that girl in Honolulu?"

"He is a violent man. Passionate. But he is also pretty smart."

"If he didn't kill the girl, who else had any reason to?"

"How can I help you? I was not there."

"Would Elizabeth Cunningham have any reason to set up Max Rolfe on a murder charge?"

"She would do it if it was necessary. She would not think, she would just do it. But why is it necessary?"

"The Cunninghams seem well fixed financially," I said. "You live here, if there was anything wrong you'd have some idea."

"I know he has trouble with his business. Many times his directors and accountants come here to see him and they talk for many hours. He looks worried when they leave. But they still pay all the bills."

I finished my coffee. "Okay Helga, it looks this way. I think Elizabeth Cunningham wants Max Rolfe out of the way. Not dead, just out of circulation. I don't know why but I don't trust her, I think she knows something about Honolulu – why would she have kept me here and quizzed me so hard? She wanted to know what I knew and she wouldn't do that out of idle curiosity. There's a feeling in my water that if she didn't set up the killing in Honolulu, she certainly knows something about it. Rolfe must have got wind there was something on, so he in turn set me up. I was ideal – a stranger in town, not an American, and having some association with the ways of criminals."

"But Peter, what good would it do to have him in jail? Does it have to be something to do with Mrs. Cunningham? He has many enemies . . ."

"Two things," I said. "Yesterday afternoon in this apartment she worked me over, she dragged out of me every little fact she could about that night in Honolulu. All she wanted to know was what happened in Honolulu – and she wanted to know it all, every minute detail. No woman does that, no woman goes to such – extremes – for the sake of a passing interest in a former husband. She has got to be involved."

"And the other thing?"

"At the party in Honolulu before the girl was killed, Rolfe made a special point of telling me about his wife." I stopped and considered that for a moment. "He deliberately put me in the position of the patsy, and he also deliberately told me about his wife. He knew enough about me to be pretty sure I'd have to follow it up to get myself off the hook, thus getting him off the hook as well. I think he pointed me at Elizabeth with a purpose. Imagine it this way: he learns his former wife has him in her sights for some reason, he learns something about my reputation and so he puts me where I have to save his neck to save my own. Neater than hiring a private agency. He keeps his hands clean. And in this case I'm less corruptible."

"But how do you prove it, Peter?"

"I find out *why* she wants him in custody."

"I wish I could help you. I do not know about these things."

"You could be more help than you imagine." I looked at my watch. "Tell the Cunninghams I'll be here for dinner."

"About six-thirty," she said. "Cocktails first."

"I'll be here."

"Peter, I will do anything to help. But you must help me."

"We have a deal."

"What can you do for me?"

"If we can squeeze Elizabeth Cunningham into a corner, perhaps we can trade with her. If not, there's always a guy – somewhere – who's going to owe me a lot by the time I'm through in New York, one way or another."

"I will keep you to your word."

I laughed. "Oh boy – I know you will. Now I have to move. I'll see you tonight."

I waved down a cab and as the driver battered his way through the late Sunday afternoon traffic back to my hotel, I thought about the things Helga Brandt had told me. If I could stall off the Honolulu Police Department long enough, we had a chance. Slender, but still a chance.

Main problem was to sweat on the Honolulu cops not finding the dead girl's friend, the one who had spent such a short and busy time in the Reef Hotel with me. If they found her, and if she talked, and if she remembered who I was, they might have just enough evidence to want me back in Hawaii for questioning.

And then I knew they'd found her. The cab stopped outside my hotel and I could see through into the brightly illuminated foyer. I caught a brief glimpse of Detective Frank Pagnucco of the D.A.'s office leaving the reception desk to talk with two uniformed patrolmen.

The hotel doorman hadn't reached the cab yet. I told the driver, "Keep driving, I changed my mind. Just keep driving ahead."

I didn't have to say it twice. He swung off into the Park Avenue traffic and headed downtown. The hotel doorman hadn't seen me.

The driver asked, "Where to now, mister?"

"Anywhere."

He turned right at the next cross street.

"You in some kind of trouble?"

"I've just got time to kill."

"I don't want no trouble in my cab."

"I'm in no trouble."

"Uh huh."

70

He used his right hand to fill in a form clipped to a board near the wheel. He said, carefully, "I still got to fill in my log, you know that."

"How much?"

He took a quick look at me through his rear-vision mirror. "I guess a twenty should cover it."

I gave him the twenty. "Now just keep driving."

"Okay."

I shouldn't have asked him how much; ten would probably have bought silence and a log record that wouldn't trace me. But this was no time to put a discount price on my freedom to move.

Time was running short for me. I reckoned on making dinner with the Cunninghams but after dinner I would become a foreign fugitive from local justice and possibly New York's best-dressed homeless person. I wouldn't even have a suitcase. It would have been warmer in a Honolulu jail.

Chapter 17

"You an Englishman, mister?" The cab driver's name was Fulton J. Schultz. It was displayed with his photograph on the licence panel in front of me.

"No, Australian," I said.

"You talk like an Englishman."

"An Englishman would be shocked."

"Funny people, the English. I had a Limey shot himself in my cab once."

"I'll try to be careful."

"I picked him up near the New York Central building. Said he wanted to go out to Kennedy Airport. No luggage. So I'm driving him over the Triborough Bridge – and there I am, smack in the middle of the bridge, and bang! I look around and he's shot himself. Dead already. Right smack in the middle of the Triborough Bridge."

"What did you do?"

"He said he wanted to go out to JFK, so I took him to JFK."

"Right out to the airport ?"

"To the Port Authority police. I told them, I got this fare in back and he's dead. They said it's not their department. If it happened on the Triborough Bridge I should drive him back to a precinct station in Queens. So I do that and they don't want no part of him either. He's a mess. I never knew an Englishman could bleed so much. They say if it happened on the Triborough Bridge, I should take him to a Manhattan precinct."

"Don't tell me – they didn't want him either."

"The bridge connects between Manhattan and Queens, see, and nobody wants him and I still got him dead there in back. The Triborough goes right over Randalls Island only there's no precinct station there."

"You tried the water police ?"

"Don't make jokes, I'm losing money on this Limey. So I get back into Queens, I figure he shot himself on the Queens side of the toll gates, and I stop on Astoria Boulevard. I see this patrolman and I tell him I'm going to dump the body on the sidewalk. He can book me for a litterbug if he wants. So then they got to do something. He calls in and his captain makes an executive decision. They'll take the body. They didn't like it. Made me wait an hour for the meat wagon. Then I call my boss and he says, did I get the fare."

"Did you ?"

"Listen, I had to pay even the carwash out of my own pocket."

"It's a cruel world."

"Point I'm making is, you can drive around this town all day with me and there ain't nobody going to even *want* to know about you. No radio. They can't put out a call and ask has anybody seen this guy who talks like a Limey. You can sit in this cab with me all day and all night. Fifteen cents the first quarter mile and five cents every quarter mile after. Plus tips."

"Have you ever had anybody pay you to drive around all night so he can sleep in the back ?"

"I've had every other kind of fare. Had a guy just bought a Sterno stove, he tried to light it up in back and make toast. Tell you what I'm going to do. You want to sleep in back is all right with me, I'll give you a special price. I'll waive the tip. It's a slow night."

"Sounds like an expensive flophouse but I'll keep it in mind.'

72

I looked at my watch. "Head for the East Seventies, I have a dinner date."

"Man. Here's a guy, he dines out in the East Seventies and he sleeps in a cab."

"I'll try to avoid that if I can. You won't forget the twenty I gave you?"

"Only fare I ever put in was a dead one, mister. You'll be okay."

And I reflected that cab drivers around the world speak an international language but that one day, of them all, the New York cab driver would rule the earth.

I told the doorman who I was and he checked on the security phone then ushered me to the elevator. I'd have liked to have had a shower and changed, but I would have to hope the Cunninghams might think that not washing was an eccentric Australian habit.

Helga opened the door for me.

"Good evening, Mr. Heysen. Can I take your coat?" I slipped my coat off and she took it, and with a quick movement of her hand she put a fold of paper into my jacket pocket, letting me see it first.

"Mr. and Mrs. Cunningham are in the next room, Mr. Heysen. Would you come this way?"

"Thank you." I felt my pocket to be sure the paper she had passed me wasn't showing. I wondered when I would have a chance to read it.

"Peter. I'm glad you could come. Darling, this is Peter Heysen, the friend of Max's I was telling you about."

We were in the main living room of the Cunningham apartment, with all the gilt-framed paintings of men on horseback and plump young girls with pale faces and red cheeks. Elizabeth wore a loosely-cut magenta dress with a high halter neck; loosely-cut, yes, but cut from the kind of fine, soft synthetic fabric that clings wherever it can, and it did. She swooped me up and hustled me across the deep carpet to shake hands with John Cunningham.

He was a small, frail old man, much smaller than his wife, with silver-grey hair and pale grey eyes. He stood erect, so erect he was almost leaning back, and he punched out his hand. "Glad to meet you, Peter, glad to meet you."

"Glad to meet you, Mr. Cunningham."

"First names. You're Peter, I'm John. Okay?"

73

"Okay."

His voice put a lie to his looks: he might seem fragile but his voice was strong, to the point. And at a second look I saw his protruding jaw, the straight set of his mouth, and the intelligence in his eyes. He was an old man but a tough and pretty vigorous one by the looks of him.

Elizabeth said, "I'm really glad you could come at such short notice, Peter. I think you should see just how happy John and I are together. Isn't that right, John?"

"Of course. Martini, Peter?"

"Thanks."

"Elizabeth told me you had some story about Rolfe saying we weren't happy together. Couldn't be happier, Peter. Crazy, I suppose – old guy like me with an attractive young woman like Elizabeth. But I've got a lot more stamina than I might appear to have – right, Elizabeth?"

"Right, darling." She giggled. She actually giggled. She looked like she might even blush.

"Well," I said, "that's about what Elizabeth told me. Remember, Max Rolfe isn't a friend of mine, just an acquaintance. I've merely reported to Elizabeth what he told me."

John Cunningham handed me a martini. "We're not too worried about Max Rolfe," he said. "Man's a fool. He should never have lost Elizabeth. That was his mistake. I capitalised on it. Martini okay?"

"Fine thanks."

"Sit down, sit down." We all sat down, Elizabeth perched demurely on the edge of her seat beside her husband.

He said, "I understand Rolfe is in some kind of trouble. Killed a girl, something like that?"

"Elizabeth told you, then?"

"Sure. Doesn't surprise me. Had to get himself into trouble some time. Tried to involve you too, right?"

"That's right."

"Shifty character. You wouldn't think he'd bother killing the Lee girl. Just an island girl. Kill a business competitor, I wouldn't put that past him. But not some insignificant Hawaiian kid."

"How did you know her name, John?"

He looked at Elizabeth and she looked at me. "You must have told me, Peter."

"I did?"

74

"How else would I know?"

"True enough." I took a good swallow of my martini. I knew I hadn't told her the girl's name. It was about the only thing I hadn't told her.

Elizabeth was still looking at me, smiling so sweetly, the ideal hostess. "Did you find your lighter, Peter?"

I took another good swallow of my martini and glanced across at John Cunningham. He dead-panned it, his expression told me nothing. Elizabeth's question deliberately told me too much.

"Why do you ask, Elizabeth?"

"Oh, I just wondered. Whatever it was you were looking for, you found it?"

I stirred the olive in my glass. "Your maid was very helpful, Elizabeth."

"But she always is, Peter. I'm sure you discovered that?"

John Cunningham broke in: "This your first visit to New York, Peter?"

I was happy for the conversation to switch. I made small talk with him through three more martinis and Elizabeth said hardly a word; she watched me, and smiled at me, and made sure my glass was full.

When Helga came in to say dinner was ready, I escaped to the bathroom to read Helga's note. It was very straightforward and left me in no doubt at all:

"She knows you were with me today. Doorman told her. I am so sorry Peter! I had to tell her everthing we said. Please understand. I am always afraid of her. I am so sorry. What can I do?

Chapter 18

It was a great dinner, one of those memorable meals. Elizabeth and I sat facing each other, each knowing that the other knew too much now and there wasn't much either could do about it, and John sitting between us at the head of the table knowing ... knowing how much?

Helga skipped in and out with the food, the fright plain on

her face. Elizabeth was kindly and charming to her and the sweeter she smiled the more Helga shrank.

I tried several times to catch Helga's eye – thinking, desperately, that I must reassure her – and each time she carefully avoided seeing me and Elizabeth just smiled and smiled and continued smiling like the gracious hostess until I wanted to wrap the silver candelabra around her blonde head.

John Cunningham seemed oblivious to the electricity between the two women and myself. He talked on and on about television programming–if you work anywhere close to the industry you have to cop that one every so often, every man is his own expert program manager – and he and I made all the usual cracks about the commercials.

"I imagine your company uses TV in a big way, John?"

"For our retail lines we sponsor two of the highest-rating shows."

"You watch them yourself?"

"All rubbish. But they deliver the market, the great unwashed. I don't take an active role in the business anymore. Our local plant's over in Jersey, I never see it. We have a downtown office, I spend my days there but I let the younger guys run the business. I guess they must know what they're doing."

"You must've seen a lot of changes in the meat-packing business?"

"Sure. It's different now, I couldn't do it all over again, the laws are different today. I started in Arizona, worked in a slaughter house when I was a kid, by the time I was twenty-one I owned it. Bought out a small packing corporation, went on up from there. Long way from Arizona to Manhattan. Early religious training kept me going, kept my mind untroubled. Father was a tough old man, he was in groceries. Never gave me a red cent till he died and by then I was a millionaire anyway. He worked hard and he lived clean. Funny thing, I still say my prayers – every night I go down on my knees and give my thanks." He stared at me firmly. "Even give my thanks for Elizabeth here."

"She's a real prize."

Elizabeth gushed. "Really, John . . ."

"It's the truth, Peter. I'm a lucky man to have a good-looking woman like Elizabeth at my age."

"Early religious training, eh John?"

He grinned. "And some gentle persuasion. You know, she

76

was still in love with Max Rolfe when I met her. But I believe any man can get anything by argument and negotiation. Maybe I'm before my time but the unions are learning it and management is learning it. Negotiate, Peter. Sit down and argue, you'll win your point. That's how I won Elizabeth."

Elizabeth giggled. "You make it sound an awfully dull courtship, John." She looked at me. "But it was fun. He took me to all the museums and art galleries and made me see there was more to life than jetting about all over the place."

"Always liked beautiful things," John Cunningham said.

"You've collected a few," I said, pointing to the heavy paintings filling the walls.

"I collect a lot of things, Peter. After dinner I'll show you my military collection. I was never able to serve my country in uniform but I was always interested in army life. I've put together a few things."

"Stilettos," Elizabeth said, "and blunderbusses and old Confederate rifles. I think they remind you of the slaughter-house, John."

"Now that's unfair of you, Elizabeth. But it's wrong of me to expect a woman to understand, right Peter?"

"Right. Tell me John, now that you've moved up to let the younger men run your business, do you think it's still as healthy as it always was?"

He looked at me quickly, a shade too quickly. It was a deliberately rude question but his expression showed momentary shock rather than anger. "Why sure it is, sure it is. Why not? These young guys today with their law training and letters after their names, they don't do things my way . . . but they still like to make money the way I did. Business is good, Peter – very good." He wiped his lips. "If you've finished, come on up to my study, I'll show you all those old stilettos and blunderbusses."

Though the apartment was in a modern building, John Cunningham had plainly gone to considerable expense to have the walls lined with old hand-hewn and polished timber and to have adzed roof beams strung across the ceiling. No doubt from some old eighteenth-century home, he had salvaged a large ornamental fireplace with a carved wood mantel. No fire. Just an unobtrusive environment control dial by the door. Anyway, there wouldn't be any chimneys. But still it was a fine fireplace.

The walls hung with old guns, knives, helmets, pistols and other paraphernalia of carnage and destruction. An odd collection for a man who believed so deeply in the power of argument and negotiation.

Helga brought us our coffee and we smoked cigars while he showed me each piece and lovingly detailed its history. We drank many brandies.

He held an old silver-handled .38 revolver, relic of the Wild West. With his finger through the trigger guard he spun it like the movie cowboys then sighted it at a spot on the wall.

"This nonsense about Max Rolfe, Peter. Did he really kill that girl, do you suppose?"

"I don't know, John."

"Elizabeth tells me he was alone in the room with her when you arrived and she was already dead."

"That's true."

"Well, if that's not damaging evidence, what is?"

"Damaging, John – but not totally convincing."

"Why not? Goddamit, Peter, he was alone in the room with her."

"What was his motive?" I asked.

"Motive? How would I know about motive? You met him, he has motives for doing things that no normal, rational man could comprehend. Any court would have to accept that."

"You weren't there, John. I was. I seriously don't think . . ."

"Tell you what I don't get. You walk into his room, you find him with a dead girl, and you don't wait around to tell the police. It was an open and shut case for them."

"John, I knew him long enough to be careful. Perhaps having my own crime show makes me doubly cautious but I knew he had made a point of leaving me alone in that room – so it followed logically that if he would do that much, he could easily have set up other booby traps for me if I'd done the simple thing and talked to the police. I was high on booze and sex and there was a cadaver in the room and I'd already made one false move in letting him get away from me. I was in no state to be claiming my innocence to strange cops with no friends in town to vouch for what a respectable, decent-living bloke I really am. I could see only one course of action – to clear out before the roof fell in. Somebody called in the cops, and whoever did that expected the cops to find either me or Rolfe or both of us in that room. I didn't want to wait around for something else to happen to me. You said yourself that Rolfe does things no normal, rational man could comprehend."

"But you could fight that! A good lawyer . . ."

"Fight it, John? Spend weeks, perhaps months in Honolulu trying to clear myself from who knows what kind of trap he might have arranged? No thanks, I like my freedom. At the time it seemed I had more chance of keeping it if I simply disappeared. Had I stayed I could have wound up as some kind of accessory to the fact. My only chance is to get to Max Rolfe, get to the bottom of it all."

"But a good lawyer could do that for you."

"I didn't like the risk at the time. The odds might have been too severely stacked against me. Now it's too late, I'm in too deep."

"If you're worried about the cost of a good criminal attorney, maybe I could help you."

"Why, John?"

He had been sighting the revolver at various imaginary targets about the room. Now he cocked it and pointed it right at me.

"I'm tired of that bastard Rolfe making trouble."

"He's made trouble for you before?"

"He makes trouble for everybody. He's bad news. You'd think he'd leave us alone but ever since I married Elizabeth he's been a part of our lives. He deserves to be put away."

"Have you got anything on him, John?"

He waved the revolver vaguely towards me. I wanted to believe it was an absent-minded gesture but I watched it closely nevertheless. He said, "You could have him put away."

"How, John?"

"You could go to the police and tell them all you know . . ."

"Sure, and get myself in more strife . . ."

"I'll get the attorney for you, I'll fix that end of it."

"Are you bargaining with me, John?"

"I'd like to see Rolfe someplace where he can't harm anybody. You're the man to do it."

I looked down at the revolver jabbing towards my stomach to accent his words. I could see the round lead noses of bullets peeping out of the chamber.

"No John," I told him. "If Max Rolfe goes down he'll take me with him. He wouldn't rest until he had me, if I let him down." I moved to one side, out of range of the aimless revolver. I explained, "It's a theory of mine: he forced me into this in order to get himself out. If I fail, that's tough. But if I just walk in and tell my story to the nearest cop, my problems will only be beginning."

"Peter, I want you to do as I tell you."

"John – that gun is loaded." Perhaps he was trying to scare me and then again perhaps he was just clumsy with firearms, but I was tired of dodging around the room. "Put the gun down, please John."

He looked down at it and back up to me. "I know what I'm doing," he said, and then I knew he had been trying to make me sweat. But he pointed the gun away from me and uncocked it and replaced it on its wall rack.

"I'm telling you for your own good, Peter. I'll get the lawyer. We'll destroy him in court. I'll make it worth your while."

"You will?"

"How much do you expect to get out of this, if you dig deep enough to clear him?"

"I have a deal in mind."

"So do I. Do we talk cash?"

"You really do want him put inside, don't you? Even if he's innocent. Perhaps – especially if he's innocent?"

John Cunningham flashed me a quick glance of anger. "Are you saying you think I'm a part of this? You think I have something to do with that Honolulu business?"

"You're very keen to have a cage around him."

"Goddamit, Peter . . ." His face was flushed and he bunched his fists. Then slowly he relaxed, visibly taking command of himself. He crossed the room and picked up our brandies and brought me mine and I watched him as he sipped at his and finally he spoke:

"I'm sorry if I gave a bad impression of myself, Peter. I have no real reason for wanting any harm to come to Max Rolfe. No *real* reason. I just don't like him. If he's done something wrong that can be pinned on him, I want him to get his comeuppance. But I certainly had nothing to do with the things that happened in Honolulu."

"I apologise for suggesting it, John. I got mad for a moment.'

He smiled. "I guess I was riding you. I'm sorry, Peter. You see – Elizabeth is kind of scared of him. Particularly now he says he's coming to New York. For her sake it seemed the best thing. For the peace of our marriage."

"I understand."

"I sure hope you don't think either of us would have anything to do with . . . I mean, none of it's any of our business. We're just as well out of it."

"Of course."

"But if there's anything we can do to help you . . ."

"Thanks, John."

"I hope I didn't insult you, offering money like that."

"That's never an insult, John."

He smiled again. "You're my kind of man, Peter Heysen. We shake on it?"

We shook on it. He said, "Great. Let's forget I said anything, right?"

"Right."

There was a light tap at the door and Elizabeth entered, stirring a glass of warm milk.

She said, "Did I hear you two shouting?"

He laughed. "Forget it, honey. Friendly little man-to-man disagreement about nothing."

He tossed his brandy back and finished it and took the glass of milk from Elizabeth.

"Thanks, honey."

He swallowed it quickly, grimaced, and handed her the glass. "I have trouble sleeping," he told me. "Take the stuff in milk. Tastes putrid. Have another brandy?"

"Thanks."

Elizabeth asked, "When will you gentlemen be joining me? I thought Peter was my guest, John."

"Sure. Of course."

"I should be leaving," I said. "This has been an interesting evening but I mustn't stay all night. Anyway, there's so much to see in New York I don't want too many late nights."

"Wise of you, Peter. Reckon I might get off to bed. You remember what I told you about Max Rolfe. He can't harm us. You don't mind if I leave you to the tender care of my wife? Elizabeth, you keep his brandy topped up now. You let him stay as long as he likes. You won't think I'm rude, Peter?"

"Of course not, John. Thanks for showing me all this."

"I'll get off to bed then. Been a long day for an old guy. Nice to meet you, Peter."

We shook hands again and Elizabeth ushered me towards the spiral staircase. I excused myself, said I'd be with her in a moment, and ducked into the bathroom. I used the back of Helga's note to scrawl a note of my own. Somehow I had to get it into her hands.

But she was thinking ahead of me. The door eased open and she slipped into the bathroom to join me.

"You always join the guests in the bathroom ?" I asked her.

"Peter, it is not funny. The doorman . . ."

"Yes, you said so in your note."

"I am sorry. How can I say it ?"

"You really are scared of her, aren't you ?"

"It has always been that way between us. She could make too much trouble. What could I do ?"

"It's too late now. I'll help you if I can, Helga. Let me think about it. I've got problems of my own right now."

"What is it ?"

"The foyer of my hotel is probably jammed with the New York constabulary. Honolulu must've given the word they want me."

"What will you do ?"

"I've got to stay around another day or so. Once they get me back in Honolulu I can't do anything."

"Peter . . . I think I know a place."

"On a seat on the subway ?"

"Please do not be nasty. I want to help you."

"Sorry."

"Here." She took the paper and pen from me and wrote down a phone number. "This is the number of a girl I know. She will be home tonight, I hope. She is a friend. When you leave here, call her. Perhaps she can let you stay for the night and I could come and see you tomorrow. If you keep Mrs. Cunningham talking, I will call her now and I will ask her. When you leave here, call her and she will tell you what to do."

"You're sure ? You're in trouble already, and if they find you helped a fugitive . . ."

"Could it be worse ?"

"Thanks, Helga. I'll see you there tomorrow ?"

"Yes."

"Good. Now get out of here. It wouldn't surprise me if our lady friend had the bathroom bugged for sound and vision."

I tucked the paper deep into my jacket pocket and strolled casually downstairs to join Elizabeth Cunningham. Keep her talking, Helga had said. Okay then.

Chapter 19

"It's not every host," I said, "who goes to bed and leaves the guest with the hostess."

She handed me my brandy. "You said yourself, Peter, this is a sophisticated town."

"Was it a sleeping drug you gave him, Elizabeth?"

"Yes."

"Really?"

"Don't be so obvious, Peter, of course it was a sleeping drug."

"That must slow him down. He led me to believe your sex life together was pretty good."

"Good God, you can be crude when it suits you!" And then she grinned. "You don't think I'd marry a pendulous old man like John Cunningham for his sex appeal, do you?"

"Money," I said.

"Let's be more subtle about it," she said. "Call it marriage for comfort. I like John, I genuinely like him, he's a sweet old man. I give him all the pleasure that's good for him. Does he look unhappy?"

"He must really trust you, Elizabeth."

"But you don't, do you?"

I drank some of my brandy. She had carefully not taken me back into her little room. We sat facing each other across the larger sitting room. I said, "You both seem to know a lot more about Honolulu than I told you."

"Yes, John slipped up there, letting you know the girl's name. It's unlike him. But you see we had it all investigated. As soon as you told me, John called his people in Hawaii and they found out as much as they could and cabled him this morning."

"Max Rolfe must have you worried."

"He worried you, didn't he? Did you know he's in New York?"

"Where?"

"I don't know where's he's staying but I know he's here. Never mind how I heard. I think he's here for a showdown."

83

"Why do you say that?"

"You said yourself, he wants me to leave John."

"It's more than that, isn't it, Elizabeth?"

She looked at me innocently, all smiles. So I told her, "Elizabeth, it's my business – my job – to smell out more than there seems. And right now, with you, it's in my own personal interest to know. A Honolulu jail wouldn't be too unpleasant but I'll be happier if I can avoid it. I want to know why I got tangled up in a very simple case of murder. I want to know why, and to whom, it is so important that Max Rolfe should be locked away. I'd lay money you were outside that door listening, you heard John make me a cash offer – I'd go so far as to put money down that it was all your idea. I'm going to find out who and what is behind it all, one way or the other."

"Is there any good reason why I should tell you, Peter?"

"There is, and you know it."

She stood and crossed the room and looked through into the dining room and through to the kitchen. She closed the door softly and returned to her seat. She said, "Max picked the right man when he brought you into this – I'm surprised he conned you in so easily. I'm going to have to tell you, aren't I? Because of what you know about Helga and Bonifacio?"

"I'm glad you understand."

"I don't suppose," she said, "that it would be easy for them, but if the police and the insurance detective had your story about Helga and me . . . I imagine they'd find proof eventually."

"They'd break Helga down," I said. "She is your weak link. If they confronted her with the facts, she'd finally admit it. She'd know they were going to deport her anyway, she'd have nothing to lose."

"That's why I've always been stuck with her – if I'd tried to have her sent out of the country, she'd have talked."

"I know. You've been kind of glued to each other."

"I should have done something more drastic about Helga long ago," she said.

"You can't now, Elizabeth. If anything happens to Helga, I'll know about it."

She topped up our glasses and sat down again. She sipped her brandy slowly, thoughtfully. Finally she spoke.

"I was born in South Carolina," she said, "but everybody leaves South Carolina. I went to California to find me a husband. Bonifacio wasn't a rich man – hell, he was only a teacher of fabric design. But he had more than I was used to. And you know, I think I actually loved him when I married him. But when he started bringing other girls back to the apartment . . . I suppose I should've left him but it was nice to have money to buy clothes and live in a clean apartment."

"So you stayed around just long enough to milk him for alimony."

"Do you blame me? He brought his first girl home two months after we married. I was going to speech classes to get rid of my South Carolina accent and I got home just as the girl was leaving. He said she was a student. And she was just the first one. Still, I got Bonifacio's insurance money, worth a lot more to me than his lousy little monthly payments would have been."

"And you came East."

"For ten years, Peter Heysen, I have lived surrounded by big money. Not much of it has been mine, just what I could pick up on the side. But after ten years of it – and with the memory of Bonifacio to help you along – you lose a lot of your inhibitions. There aren't too many frustrations you can't satisfy."

"But now the money's gone, I hear."

"I suspected you knew about that. John is a clever businessman but he's also too honest. He can't hold out much longer, I'd say they'll bankrupt him in about two months, maybe three."

I told her, "I know a few bankrupts who are living in financial splendour in South America."

"Not John Cunningham. I wish he would. But when John is declared bankrupt that's exactly what he will be."

"And where will that leave you, Elizabeth? Alone in the world with nothing but several thousand dollars in diamonds and a few thousand in furs?"

"Look, I'm not asking for your sympathy, Peter Heysen. I'm telling you the story you want to hear because I know you'll make more trouble if I don't." She lit a cigarette. "My only chance is some stock I still hold in some of Max Rolfe's businesses."

"Now we get to the real point," I said.

"As part of the settlement when I divorced Max, I took a lump sum payment, plus some shares. When we were married,

Max gave me a percentage in three of his businesses. He holds fifty-one per cent of the three companies I'm interested in. The other forty-nine per cent is held by me and two other shareholders. I hold a bigger slice than the other two."

"Who are they?"

"Max's first wife and his daughter by his first wife."

"A great family business," I said.

"Three companies, all of them sound but none of them big. There's a macadamia nut plantation in one of the outer islands in Hawaii, a sporting goods factory in Los Angeles and a small flight navigation instrument corporation in San Diego."

"Owned jointly," I said, "by himself, his two former wives and his daughter. What a man!"

"He doesn't really care about any of the three companies," she said. "He just keeps them healthy and keeps them solvent because of his co-owners. All of them could be bigger and could make more. I lived with Max for too long, I know his business, I know how he works."

"You aim to get control of these companies, obviously. How?"

"If Max is put out of the way for a year or two, I can do it."

"You could take over by proxy?"

"I'd have no trouble with the other two, they'd come along with me. His first wife got less out of him than I did. Between the two of us, we could sell out and settle for cash."

"Elizabeth, you're a real sweetie. Have you thought about taking over the Cunningham meat-packing business? With your brain you could build it up, milk it dry, then sell it."

"You asked me, Peter, and I told you."

"So you framed – or you tried to frame – Max Rolfe. Get him out of the way on a murder charge and you take over. What about John?"

"There's no law says I can't appoint a bankrupt as a management consultant."

"So when John gave me all that rubbish about a lawyer and making it worth my while to get Max Rolfe behind bars, you put him up to it."

"Exactly. But he didn't know why. I pleaded with him, I told him I was afraid of Max. It wasn't hard, he doesn't like Max anyway."

"Is it really the money, Elizabeth? You're still young

enough to find another wealthy patron. Isn't that more your style? Or do you hate Max Rolfe so much that you want to hurt him?"

She thought a moment. "I told you, when you've had a lot of money for a long time, there aren't many frustrations you can't satisfy. Until somebody like Max Rolfe walks out on you and the world knows you as the woman who couldn't hold Max Rolfe."

"You really do hate him."

"I know I'm no paragon, Peter. But I was faithful to Bonifacio. All the while he was two-timing me under my nose, I was faithful to him. I was faithful to Max too, for a long time after I knew he was playing around. I didn't play myself until it was near the end. It's not that I hate Max, I couldn't feel that strongly about him. I just want to hurt him a little."

I pushed my brandy aside. Suddenly I didn't want to drink anymore. I said, "Max must have some inkling of this. He set me up to cop the punch for him."

"Yes. I'm sorry he did that."

"You're not sorry for my sake, Elizabeth."

"No. It's just that by bringing you in he complicated things. It was all perfectly planned. If he hadn't got you involved the police wouldn't be looking for you, they'd have dug a little deeper and gone looking for Max."

"Who did the job for you, Elizabeth?"

"A man I can trust. One of the few men I can trust because I pay him. Those diamonds and furs you talked about, there aren't many of them left."

"You're smart enough to know this makes you an accessory to murder?"

"I may have been already with Bonifacio."

"That's what I like about you, Elizabeth. You're so feminine and warm-hearted."

"Bonifacio taught me about being feminine and warm-hearted. Look, I'll tell you how warm-hearted I am. There's a man in Honolulu right now, trying to track down the other girl who was with you. They stick together, these girls. Not one of them would say who was with you. But if the other girl can be found and persuaded to talk, that should get you off the hook. The police can't find out who she was. We're trying to find out for you. You see, I want you to be cleared, it doesn't do me a scrap of good if the police get you. I want them to get Max."

"That's thoughtful of you, Elizabeth, but now that I know – what are you going to do about me? How do you stop me walking out of here and giving your story to the police after all? It should put me in a good bargaining position with them. They're looking for me, do you know that? I think they may have found the other girl already – and I think all it did was convince them I know more than I'm telling. Why don't I just go now and tell them? They'll be a little angry that I ducked them – but if I can tell them about you, that might sweeten them a little."

She stood up. I rose to follow her out to the entrance foyer. She gave me my coat and I slipped it on. "Well?" I asked her. "Why not?"

"You won't say anything about me to the police," she said. "You know you can't prove it. They won't believe you. All I have to do is deny everything. They can't trace the murder back to me. They can't prove it any more than you can. You won your point, you made me tell you, but now we're at a stalemate because there's nothing you can do about it. I suggest, Peter, that what you should do now is keep out of the way. I'll get Max. And when I get him, you'll be in the clear."

"Elizabeth, you know I won't do that."

She opened the door for me. "I think you will. I think I have a way of persuading you that whatever you say to the police, they won't believe it. I have a way of discrediting you to where they won't even bother listening."

"How's that, Elizabeth?"

She leaned forward and kissed me softly on the lips. Her kiss was cold. "You're a nice man, Peter Heysen. Don't make me do it."

I was outside the door now. I looked at her. She was indeed a very beautiful woman. She had a beautiful body. She had a way of making love that had sent me almost out of my mind. And she was a bitter, sick woman.

"Say goodnight to John for me," I said.

"I will. It was so good of you to come, Peter, and I did enjoy your company." And she closed the door gently.

Chapter 20

A little over twenty-four hours previously, I had stumbled out of the Cunningham apartment and down the elevator out into the cold on Fifth Avenue. I was just as drunk this time. But, as before, I reeled more under the impact of Elizabeth Cunningham, than the effects of cognac brandy.

I stood for a moment just outside the light of the apartment building canopy, gathering my thoughts. I needed time to think, time to reflect on what had happened and what I had learnt. In my pocket there was a note with a phone number on it but first I wanted to walk in the clear cold night and think.

With my collar turned up I walked against the wind on Fifth Avenue, with the darkness of Central Park on my left. I walked briskly and a man passed me going the other way, heavily rugged against the cold, a hat pulled down firmly over his face. I walked on, my mind tracing back over the past few days: the casually calculating manner in which Elizabeth Cunningham had outlined her plans, and the equally calculating way she had used her body to persuade me to talk the previous evening; the slow but deliberate search that had plainly gone on in Honolulu and was just as certainly going on now in New York for a man who could assist the police in the case of Sandy Lee; the case with which I had fallen sucker to Max Rolfe's play in Honolulu and the simple beginnings it had had on the terrace of the Moana Hotel watching the blue water of Waikiki and the long brown limbs of a girl from Utah . . .

I stopped and turned and looked back. Utah. Jug Ears. Maybe it was just my mind. I was losing it slowly. Or had it been him? I searched the darkness of the street but the man had gone. His hat had been pulled very low over his face and he had looked away from me as we passed. I hadn't seen him ahead of me yet suddenly he had been there. He must have stepped out of the shadows in the park. Now there was no sign of him. A couple of teenagers walked so tightly enveloped in each other they might have been a four-legged topcoat. An old Negro lady with a string bag. And a few cars.

I broke into a trot, back to the Cunningham apartment

building. The doorman, in long blue coat and peaked hat dripping with gilt, stood inside the closed glass storm doors, lighting a cigar. The elevator doors were closed but from where I stood I couldn't see if the elevators were moving or not.

The doorman looked up and saw me; the same doorman who had told Elizabeth Cunningham I had spent most of the afternoon with her maid. No doubt she provided the cigars, probably smuggled in from Havana. I stepped back into the dark, into the night, and started walking again.

Rolfe had said, "I'm going to get Elizabeth away from that s.o.b."

And, "You wait here, I'll call my cop friend on a pay phone outside."

John Cunningham had said, "Business is good, Peter – very good."

And Elizabeth had told me, "A man in jail can't stay in business, Peter."

"I got Bonifacio's insurance money."

"The other forty-nine per cent interest is held by me and two other shareholders."

"It's not that I hate Max . . . I just want to hurt him a little."

"You know you can't prove it. They won't believe you. All I have to do is deny everything."

She may have been right when she said it was stalemate. I knew about her insurance fraud, enough about it to have the Bonifacio enquiry re-opened and probably put Elizabeth in custody and Helga on the next ship back to Germany. It was information I could use to hurt Elizabeth but I couldn't use it without hurting Helga as well, and I needed Helga. And even more to the point, it wouldn't help me much; I would still be in trouble over the death of Sandy Lee.

I could go to the police and tell them what I knew of Elizabeth's desperate plans. I knew she meant it and that if anybody was ruthless enough and determined enough to carry it off, she was.

But she would smile at the investigating officers, she would introduce them to her respected husband, and the investigating officers would remind each other that I had been in the Reef Hotel with the dead girl and they would apologise to Mr. and Mrs. Cunningham for bothering them and they would chain me to the wing of the first plane to Hawaii.

For all the information I had, I still had no proof of anything beyond the fact that I was in a strange, cold city, being sought by the police.

I had only two likely friends in the whole city, one of whom – Dave Angove – I could not involve because he had a job to hold down and couldn't afford to have his reputation come under suspicion, and anyway he was probably already being watched, and the other of whom – Helga – was probably too afraid to do more than give me a place to hide for a night.

Well, it was a cold night. At least I could get warm there. Or so I had hoped but even that small pleasure had to wait.

"Why did you nearly go back to her apartment, old friend? Want to lay her again?"

I swung around. He had come up beside me quietly. Max Rolfe. Tall, blond, his suntan no doubt a couple of days fresher than mine was. Anger hit me at the sight of him; I stared at him, the sudden fury moving from my head to my gut to my fists. I hurled one sharp jab into his stomach and as he lurched back against the wall surrounding Central Park I swung another at him. He blocked it.

"Hey, take it easy!"

I stood off. I wanted to hit him again and it took me a second or more to find words. "I owe you more than that, Max."

"Okay, but not here, all right? Take a slow look over your shoulder. That way."

I stepped further back, ready for him, and I threw a quick glance to the other side of Fifth Avenue. A patrolman stood under a street light, swinging his long night stick in his left hand, watching us.

"I parked the car a block back and followed you. You and I have some talking to do, I think."

"I think we just might, Max."

"So walk slowly back to the car with me. Laugh a little. We're a couple of harmless drunks. Friendly horseplay. No harm in it. Unless you want him to join us."

I looked back at the cop. I laughed, loudly and drunkenly. I cuffed Max Rolfe over the ear, playfully but a shade harder than was necessary. We threw our arms around each other like two bar-flies filled with brotherly love. We leaned on each other back to his car. I kneed him once in his leg. I slipped a little and gave him an elbow jolt to the ribs that winded him. He parried a kidney punch and laughed stupidly. Friendly

91

horseplay. We staggered into his car and as he slid behind the wheel the heel of my shoe met his shin bone. He winced.

I hissed, "Laugh, you bastard."

He laughed and stood firmly on my foot. The patrolman turned away from us and continued on his beat down Fifth Avenue. Max put the car in gear. I lit a cigarette. I was beginning to feel much better.

Chapter 21

He stopped and switched off the motor in the middle of Central Park. It was very quiet and very dark, an ideal place for a talk in complete privacy. We kept the windows wound up against the cold. Outside, the park stretched away into blackness, dimly lit by a few scattered lights. There were no other cars.

Max lit his own cigarette. He chuckled softly. "Hey, Peter Heysen, now that was real mean of you. You could hurt a guy."

"I'm working on it," I said.

"Now look, I know I spoilt a nice quiet vacation for you. But I needed your help . . ."

"I could hardly refuse."

"You saw the trouble I was in. I had to get out of there, they had me in a corner."

"So you let me take it for you."

"You're taking the strain okay."

"Jesus, I should've killed you back there, right under the eyes of that patrolman. You're about to take the strain off me, Max."

"Glad to, old friend. What've you found out for me?"

"Is that why you let me take all your punishment, because you didn't know . . . ?"

"I didn't know, I still don't know. Somebody wants me in police trouble, they want me out of the way. In London a month ago the police found a girl beat-up in my hotel room. She claimed I did it to her. I was with another broad in another hotel, but they never found her. She was my alibi and she went into smoke. Catch was, these Scotland Yard cops are good, they could smell something wrong and they worked over the beat-up girl until she admitted she'd been paid money to get a little bruised then lie down and cry help in my room. She didn't know who paid her, just a guy with big ears."

"Jug Ears."

"You know him?"

"He was sitting at the next table when you met me at the Moana."

"Are you sure?"

"You don't remember he had big ears?"

"Hell, Peter, I don't go around looking at ears, I got other things to look at."

"Too bad. We both should have looked more closely at him. He's a friend of your former wife Elizabeth."

"How do you know?"

"She told me. Obviously he was sitting there near us, listening to every word. He knew we were going to Davidoff's party, and that was his cue to set you up."

"How?" He was interested now.

"Jug Ears," I said, "persuaded two local girls to crash Davidoff's party. I'm sure of it. Elizabeth told me there were two girls involved . . ."

"How did she know?"

"Let me tell it my way, Max. I'd take bets he had two girls find their way into that party. I expect one was supposed to keep me busy in case I noticed too much, and the other one was supposed to work on you. No doubt he paid them enough not to question why."

"Do you know why?" he asked.

"Call it an educated guess, Max. Somebody, who shall be nameless for the moment, wants you in trouble. This person doesn't have much imagination. A beat-up girl in your London hotel room. A beat-up girl in your Honolulu hotel room. Same play, different theatre. He was probably waiting on the terrace of the girl's room at the Reef Hotel when you went in there with her. This time he wasn't taking any chances, he wanted you to be found with her. And you passed out drunk, right?"

"Bombed."

"So the man on the terrace – or in the closet or wherever the hell he was waiting – came into the room and killed the girl. Possibly he didn't mean to kill her, and then again he might have learned a lesson in London, where the girl talked too much. This time there'd be no talk. He killed her and then he made an anonymous call to the Honolulu police from an outside phone. Luckily for you, you woke up in time. Unluckily for the girl, she didn't read the fine print in her contract. You called me, you left me with the body, and you blew. Did you call the police, Max, did you really have a friend in the Police Department?"

He shook his head.

"I might have known," I said. "It had to be the killer who called them. He believed the police would find you there, smashed out of your mind with a dead lady by your side. Fortunately they found only the dead lady."

"And you say that the guy who did this was the guy with the big ears?"

"Max, if I knew that for certain I'd be talking with a man from the District Attorney's office, not with you. But anyhow, it's a far better bet than some horses I've known."

"So where is this guy now?"

"He's just a pawn, Max. You want the queen."

"How do you mean?"

"If you really want him, he's with Elizabeth right now."

"The hell he is! The bastard! What's he doing to her? I know, that creep Cunningham is behind it all . . ."

"You still don't see it, do you?"

"How's that?"

"Elizabeth is a shareholder in three of your business interests. With you out of the way she can take over, take out what she wants and sell out. She doesn't want you dead, Max, just out of action. It's revenge, Max, simple sweet revenge. I imagine she wants you to be alive to see what happens to you. A case of don't die, just suffer."

"I don't believe it. Where'd you get all this? Elizabeth is a real kook but she would never dream up a scheme like that."

"Macadamia nuts, sporting goods and flight navigation instruments."

"She told you that?"

"Could I have made it up?"

"No, she wouldn't do it. Anyhow, if she was desperate for money she'd be better off with me dead. I guess. Or would she know that? Hell, she'd know . . . or maybe she wouldn't know who I'd will the majority holdings to. No, she couldn't gamble on taking control with me dead. But with me in jail . . ."

"All your assets are frozen, right ?"

"Like that. You can't run a legit business from the State pen. A mob, a crooked union, sure. But I have deals going all over the States and in Latin America, Canada, England . . . if I went to jail I'd strike out on them all, it'd cost me." He laughed. "You know something, if you're right, Peter Heysen, she's a real smart girl. Real smart."

"You still want her back ?"

"Never said I wanted her back, just away from that Cunningham creep. You know his business is going bad ? She's got to get away from him. Maybe I always underrated her, I should take her back and have her work for me. I couldn't live with her but she could work for me."

"Max, if you're stupid enough to consider it, please do it. Anything to get me back to Honolulu for a quiet holiday."

"Yeah. Yeah, I guess that would be stupid. You're sure she set this whole deal up ?"

"With the help of Jug Ears."

"Can you prove it ?"

"Why don't you just let me off the hook – why don't you tell the police I wasn't there when Sandy Lee was killed – then you take it from here and get your own proof."

"I'd have to admit I was in the hotel room with her. I don't want to be even remotely connected with any murder."

"You'll pay me for this, Max."

"You think I don't know that ? Okay, I'm sorry I had to set you up but I had to do it, I had no option. But you're in it now and I'll make it sweet for you when it's all over."

"You bet you will. First thing you'll do is find me a place to hide out in this town for a few days while you and I track down Jug Ears. The two of us."

He looked at me and grinned. "Okay. Police got tabs on you ?"

"I think," I told him quietly, "they want me in Honolulu regarding a certain unsavoury murder there."

"Okay, don't rub my nose in it. I know a place. I'll take you there now. It's not the best part of the West Side but it's quiet and it's comfortable and it's got . . ."

But I never did hear what else it had. I heard my door coming open. I heard myself yelling once and I saw sharp splinters

95

of light and felt myself rolling and then squatting and shaking my head, and then I saw more lights, this time swimming past me in a pool of darkness. They stopped and they were the lights in Central Park, seen through long winter grass.

I lifted my head slowly. It hurt right down the back of my neck. I began to understand that I was lying on my stomach with my head twisted. I pushed myself up onto my elbows.

At first it was hard to focus down on what I saw. Then it came clearer to me. Max Rolfe, fifty feet up a slope, lying in a sprawl half in and half out of the car. He didn't move. But I could hear him breathing deeply.

And I thought, How can I hear a man breathing fifty feet away?

I turned to one side and saw the muzzle of a long-nosed automatic, probably a heavy .45 calibre. The long nose was deceptive. It was a silencer. It wouldn't help much on a big .45. My eye travelled down the barrel to the hand wrapped around the grip, and down the arm to the face at the end of it, the mouth open and breathing heavily, the ears noticeably big.

He was going to shoot me and press the automatic into the unconscious hand of Max Rolfe. The first patrolman on the scene would find Max holding a gun and me dead from a slug from that gun.

Jealous killer shoots former wife's friend, the headlines would shriek.

And back home they would say, *Peter Heysen shot dead by vicious American gunslinger*.

And all my good friends would pour another tankard down their parched throats and tell each other, *Bloody fool, he had it coming*.

Would they ship my body home or bury me here in New York?

Or Honolulu? A hell of a place to die but a nice place to be buried.

Chapter 22

I didn't pause long enough to ponder my interment at any length. I had a moment to live and only one moment.

Jug Ears had attacked two big, healthy men. Plainly he had used a good deal of force on me alone to hurl me this far down the slope away from the car. And Max Rolfe would not be an easy man to bash unconscious – especially as he must have had some kind of warning when the door burst open and I was attacked. Jug Ears was dragging the cold night oxygen into his lungs like a weary man. He had made a desperate move. Now I made mine.

I rolled over on my back and in the same movement grabbed his gun and pulled hard, jerking downwards with all my energy. The explosion shook my arms as the muzzle rammed into the earth and he fired simultaneously.

The earth here was soft, just soft enough not to split open the barrel and probably maim us both. But the shock as the gun went off tore it away from both of us as Jug Ears came down on top of me.

I brought my knee up and it hit bone. Head bone. Jug Ears rolled once and came up quickly. He was a strong man. He looked scrawny but he had long, hardened muscles in his thin frame and the suppleness of a man who has worked on it daily.

I scrambled in the darkness towards where I reckoned the gun must be and I found it and tucked it under my chest like a footballer gaining possession in the last minute of a drawn game. And he came down on me from a great height.

He had my head between two boney hands and slowly his fingers worked around to find my eyes.

My left arm was useless, knotted under the weight of the two of us. My right hand held the gun and quickly, angrily, I raised my right shoulder enough to force the muzzle out and point it in the general direction of Jug Ears's face.

He saw it and his hands came away from my head. I curled my finger around the trigger and turned to look at him.

He drew in his breath and snapped away from me.

I kept the gun on him and sprawled over on my back. He

stood away from me, his hands wide in front of himself in fright, as if to catch the bullet when it came.

I started to get to my feet and he looked about through the trees for some kind of escape.

He took off into the darkness, his heavy topcoat billowing out like a cape. I raised the gun from a kneeling position and steadied it on the wrist of my other arm and took careful aim and then I put it down again. In the poor light I checked it. The barrel was clear but in the impact of firing direct into the earth the shell had probably split in the breech; whatever the reason, the gun was so severely jammed I couldn't even remove the magazine. I stuffed it rather gingerly inside my shirt.

I stood up and listened. Jug Ears had gone, there was no sound from his direction. But the fight had aroused interest from another quarter.

I dropped into the shadows as a police patrol waggon wheeled to a stop beside Max's car. I watched as they went to him. One stayed with him while the other returned to use the radio.

It was time for me to follow Jug Ears.

They light Central Park brightly in parts but it would take searchlights and flares to chase away all the shadows. I headed across the park to the West Side and passed close to the old castle, now in darkness, where I had seen Elizabeth Cunningham for the first time. And once, against the night sky, I might have seen the flapping of a coat from the courtyard of the castle. I moved in close, the gun in my hand now, but he had gone, if he had been there at all.

I heaved the useless gun far out into the lake below the castle. It had too many of my prints all over it for it to be safely left lying about for interested cops. I scuttled back into the night.

There were sirens in the distance but they may have meant nothing; at any hour in Manhattan there are sirens in the distance.

I left the park and lost myself in the brooding shadows of the West Side's dilapidated apartment buildings, cheap hotels and more of those fire escapes. I found a pay phone and used it.

"Yes?"

"Helga Brandt said I should call . . ."

"You must be Peter. I'm on 84th Street between Central

98

Park West and Columbus. It's a walk-up apartment." She told me how to get there.

"I'll be five or ten minutes."

"Okay, I'll have a drink waiting."

It was a small apartment for a big girl. A little bed-sitting-room and bathroom, and a tiny kitchen that was more of a cupboard with a shoebox-sized cooker in it. She, on the other hand, had big breasts and thighs and long legs, a mass of long black hair and a large mouth, and hip bones like the handles of an old Greek amphora. She seemed to fill most of the apartment herself, and what space remained was hung with drying hosiery and flimsy lingerie that might have been of encouraging sensuality had it not been so oversize and I so preoccupied.

"Sorry," she said, "I've been washing all my dainties to-night. Sit down on the chair there, I'll use the bed. Here's a bourbon, push that nightie to one side so we don't have to look at each other through it, would you like more splash in your bourbon?"

"One splash is fine, thanks."

"I'm Rose Meinrath, I've known Helga since about two years. We met at a dressmaking class at the Y. Can you imagine? Dressmaking! Since then I tried sculpture and ladies' judo and music appreciation, I wonder why?"

"You have to do something with your time," I said.

"You said it, Peter! Mind if I call you Peter? Helga – she's great, isn't she? – she says I'm too familiar. But I like to be friendly. Friendly like the neighbourhood old maid, I guess. My, look at your coat, have you been in some kind of a fight?"

"Just a little one."

"There's a tailor down on the next corner, he knows me. Tomorrow he'll fix it for you, I'll tell him I want fast service, he'll have it maybe lunchtime."

"I don't want to be any bother to you, Rose."

"Bother? What's bother? Hey, I tell you, it's nice to have a man in the place. That's no bother. I'll just get into my pyjamas if you'll turn your back – thanks. I'm sorry I can't offer you anyplace but the floor to sleep on – only you're Helga's – well, I mean, she did see you first – all I can do is offer you the floor. I'll put cushions down."

"Thanks, Rose."

"Say, you tired, Peter?"

"Yes."

"Oh. Oh, well then – I better let you get some sleep."

"I'll wait up for Helga."

"Okay, maybe we can have a game of something. Scrabble or checkers maybe, while you're waiting."

"Did Helga say how long she'd be?"

"You don't want to play scrabble?"

"I'd be happy to play scrabble with you anytime . . ."

"You can turn around now, Peter. Pretty kooky, huh?"

She wore bright green paisley pyjamas, neck-to-knees, and she flopped about loosely inside them and knew it and laughed about it. "I better put on my gown," she said, "else Helga will kill me. How's your bourbon?"

"It's okay, Rose. I hope I'm not inconveniencing you . . ."

"I only ever had one man was an inconvenience. Way back when I first came to New York from Podunk. You're British, you wouldn't know where Podunk is, I guess?"

"Arkansas?"

"Further. It's nowhere, it's no place. Podunk, U.S.A. This guy, he was from Podunk too. Think of any small town not on any map and that's Podunk. We're two small town kids, we come to New York. I'm here to make it on Broadway and he figures he's here to make me. He follows me everyplace, spoiling my style. You know the kind, you can't break a suspender without he's there to fix it – with his bare hand? He was an inconvenience. Do you know Mary Jane?"

"Pot."

"Right. I smoke it sometimes, I can take it or leave it, you know. So I'm having a smoke one night and he comes in and I'm kind of high and I think, this guy I got to be rid of, so I tell him I'm smoking marihuana and he says he'd like to try it so I get to thinking, I have this parcel I bought on Broadway and it's all bad, I had a real lousy time on it, so I roll him one out of that. Boy, was he sick. He figured I'd poisoned him or something and maybe I had at that, it was real contaminated weed. Anyways, I never saw him again, he went reeling and rolling out of here, he must've crawled on hands and knees all the road back home. Tough. I never laid eyes on him again. Never made Broadway, neither. I wait tables in a Tenth Avenue bar. I guess no other guy will be an inconvenience. The story of my life. Hey, that'll be Helga."

She sprang to her feet and pushed through the lingerie jungle to open the door and Helga brought the cold night in

100

with her; she stood by the steam heater to warm herself. She took her coat off. Rose said, "I guess you two want I should leave you . . ."

"No, it's okay . . ."

"I'll use the john so's you can talk. I don't want to hear, I don't want to know. Don't let me go to sleep in there."

I looked at Helga and we both laughed. She said, "She is a funny girl but she knows many things and she is very kind. Your coat is torn, Peter, there was trouble?"

Helga sat on the bed and listened while I finished my bourbon and told her my story. I told her about Jug Ears.

"I think I have seen him," she said. "Three, perhaps four months ago a tall man – thin – with big ears – he came to the apartment. He had little eyes, much too small for him."

"That'd be him."

"I answered the door to him but Elizabeth Cunningham must have been expecting him. She came to the door and sent me back inside. She talked to him at the door and I saw her give him money. It seemed strange at the time, but you get used to strange things with Mrs. Cunningham."

"You didn't see him at the apartment tonight?"

"No. But somebody was there. I heard the security phone go and Mrs. Cunningham answered it and then she spoke to someone at the door. I did not see."

"There's not much you don't see."

She smiled. "I am not ashamed. It is necessary. I am only ashamed that I told her so much when she knew you had been with me at the apartment. But she knew so much about you, she had already guessed what you were thinking about her. What could I say? She can threaten me with so much – she knows so many important people now – and I am not even a citizen."

"Well, it's too late to cry over it, the damage is done. Tell me about John Cunningham, what does he know about his wife?"

"He does not know the things you and I know."

"Have you ever tried telling him?"

"He is an honest man, I think. But he is a fool with her. Once, I told her I would go to him and tell him things about her – but she laughed and said he would not believe."

"Is that true, do you think?"

"Yes," she said. "A year ago, one night when he was at

101

home alone and he was in a mood for talking, I told him Mrs. Cunningham had made up her mind to marry him long before he thought about it. I said it like a joke but I meant it serious, but he did not think I could be serious, he told me how hard he had to try to make her marry him. He is blind to her."

"No good me talking to him ?" I said.

"No good."

"I'm going to try it."

"It will not work, Peter."

"I'll try it anyway. Tomorrow."

"Why, Peter ?"

"She's got John Cunningham believing everything she says – even Max Rolfe won't see how dangerous she is. But if we can make Cunningham see, make him understand what kind of woman she is, then she's in real trouble. If I can convince Cunningham . . ."

"You will not do it with talk, Peter."

"I'll have to shock him into seeing what she is."

"Not with talk. I think he likes you now. But if you say anything against her, it will be harder for you."

"Hey, can I come out now ?" It was Rose.

"Sure, come on out. You didn't have to hide in there."

She came out smiling. "Wish I had another room for you two."

"It's all right," Helga said. "I will be getting back now before they miss me."

"Getting back ?" Rose asked. "What's the matter, Helga honey ?" She looked at me. "I thought you two – I mean – don't you . . . ?"

"No, we don't," I said.

"You'd make a nice couple," she said.

I told her, "It's an idea I'll work on, Rose. Tonight we just wanted to talk."

"Talk won't get you anyplace," Rose said.

Helga looked at me and smiled and I was reminded of the flash of recognition and promise that had passed between us when we first met.

She said, "I keep telling him that talk is not enough."

Chapter 23

I awoke stiff and sore, as much from the hardness of Rose's floor as from the beating I had taken that night.

I sat up slowly. It was late, nearly eleven-thirty a.m. I looked about the room. Rose had made her bed and pinned to it, facing me, was a note: "*Wait. I'll be back.*" All of my clothes except my shoes and tie had gone.

By the time she got back I had refreshed myself under a scalding hot shower, shaved myself with her razor and thrown together some breakfast.

I sat on the bed with a towel around my middle, flipping anxiously through a copy of *True Romance*.

"Hi. You must have been tired. I got your coat fixed and your trousers pressed. I took your other things to the laundromat. They sure gave me a look when I dropped in a man's undershirt and shorts." She put a big parcel beside me on the bed. "It's all in there. Did you sleep in your altogether last night?"

"Yes."

"Imagine, a naked man in my apartment!"

"What would they say in Podunk, Rose?" I grinned.

"They wouldn't believe Rose Meinrath left you alone. I hardly believe it myself."

"We missed a beautiful opportunity."

"Sure," she said wryly. "I saw how you kissed Helga when she left."

"A brotherly peck on the lips, Rose." I opened the parcel. "You needn't have done all this."

"It wasn't so much what you made with the lips, it was what you didn't mean to make with the eyes. I'm real happy you wear drip-dry shirts, I wouldn't know where to start ironing a man's shirt."

"Thanks Rose," I paid her for the laundry and for the tailor and I dressed and thanked her again and left hurriedly.

Outside, I called Dave Angove on a pay phone.

"Peter, where the hell are you?"

"You know I'm not going to tell you, Dave. Are you alone?"

"Yes. Why did you skip the hotel? Don't tell me, I know why, they told me about the murder. You shouldn't have disappeared, Peter, it makes it look bad."

"Dave, I know that. Have you heard anything of Max Rolfe?"

"He's in this too?"

"Dave, the police didn't mention him to you?"

"No, not that it means anything. If you're asking about him you must know already that he was mugged in Central Park last night."

"Yes. How is he?"

"He's okay. Satisfactory condition. Let me check now . . . he's at Lenox Hill Hospital, that's on Park and 78th."

"You're sure he's okay, then?"

"I'll check some more if you like. I only noticed it in the *Times* this morning because you were looking for his former wife. Do you want me to take a look at him?"

"You're better out of it, Dave. No, I just wanted to know if he was okay."

"I've had a blast from the home office, Peter. Laidlaw himself asking, where are you? What do I say?"

"I'm on vacation, Dave. You tell Laidlaw from me that it's none of his bloody business what I do in my own time."

"You know how much notice he'll take of that, Peter."

"Tell him anyway, Dave. I'll keep in touch with you."

"How much longer, Peter?"

"Today should see me out of it, Dave. I'm in a corner. I think I know the way out. I'll call you."

I hung up and whistled up a cab and went downtown to face John Cunningham.

His office was high in an elderly building on Sixth Avenue near 42nd Street. I announced myself to a girl at a desk and asked to see Cunningham. I had no appointment.

She accompanied me down a long corridor of offices and I noted many of them were empty and in darkness.

"Cutting back on staff?" I asked.

"Mr. Cunningham's secretary is this way, Mr. Heysen."

His secretary was a lean old lady with frills and spectacles behind an antique desk. She asked me to wait in a high-backed chair.

"Mr. Cunningham is on the phone right now, Mr. Heysen. He won't keep you long."

"Thanks. You have a lot of empty offices around here."

"Yes. We do." And she attacked her typewriter noisily, preventing any further attempt at conversation.

A buzzer sounded on her desk twice.

"Mr. Cunningham will see you now. This way, please Mr. Heysen."

His office was large and comfortable, almost as cluttered with heavy paintings as his apartment. Cunningham seemed very tiny behind a leather-topped desk. He stood up.

"Peter – I tried to call you this morning. They said you weren't at your hotel anymore."

"I moved out, John."

"Where are you now?"

"I found a better place. I'm sorry to come barging in here but I had to see you."

"I wanted to see you too. Did you have anything to do with Max Rolfe last night? I read about him in the *Times* this morning."

"You mean Max is here in New York, John?"

"Not long after you left us last night, Rolfe was attacked in the park, near our apartment. Did you have anything to do with that?"

"Me? Attack Rolfe? John, this is the first I heard he was in the city."

"You came to see us with some crazy story about Rolfe and last night he was mugged . . ."

"How is he? Does he know who it was?"

"Elizabeth and I talked it out this morning over breakfast," he said.

"And it was *her* idea I went out and found him and beat him up? Come on now, John . . ."

"You're lucky my wife thinks so highly of you, Heysen."

"Sure."

"I wanted to call the police and tell them about your visit but Elizabeth persuaded me not to. She thinks we're better out of it. I don't know. There's something going on here and I don't like the stink it makes."

"That's what I came to see you about, John. I wanted to talk to you about Elizabeth."

"She's got nothing to do with this."

"I think you jump too quickly to her defence, John. Perhaps you suspect something already?"

"Explain that." His voice was clipped and hard.

"John, how much do you know Elizabeth?"

He studied my innocent, smiling face very carefully. "You're trying to tell me something?"

"What I'm saying is, the trouble I'm in was caused by your wife."

"The hell it was! Rolfe is the man you should see!"

"John – your wife Elizabeth is an accessory to murder. She arranged the killing of that girl in Honolulu. She planned for Rolfe to take the blame. With Rolfe put away she can use her shareholding in some of his interests to take them over outright. She wants the money. She knows you're going broke."

"Godammit Heysen, that's going too far!" He bounced off his chair and strutted around the table to me.

"John, I know how it sounds ..."

"It sounds like the goddammest thing I ever heard! That's got to be libel."

"I can't prove it John, but I talked with Elizabeth last night ..."

"Of course you can't prove it. That's the craziest, goddammest thing I ever heard!"

"John, will you stop ranting on and listen to me? Sit back in your chair and hear me out. For your own sake, try to understand. Elizabeth knows your business is going bad. She reckons on taking over a part of Max Rolfe's interests – interests where she already holds a percentage ..."

"Elizabeth doesn't hold stock in any of his business. Where'd you get that story?"

"From Elizabeth herself. The only way she can get control ..."

"Crap, Heysen! What kind of line is this?"

"It was the man with big ears," I said, "who killed the girl in Honolulu. I'm sure of it. Do you know a friend of Elizabeth's with big ears? Tall, thin man."

"Sure, I know him."

"Elizabeth, I think, paid him off to kill the girl and make Rolfe the patsy. He was in your apartment last night."

"My apartment?"

"He was the one who attacked Max Rolfe."

"Ah, so you know about that after all? You must have gotten away just in time to escape the police. Do they know you were there? Did you report it to them?"

"What's his name," I asked, "this character with the big ears?"

But in answer to me, John Cunningham returned behind his desk and pressed his office intercom button. His secretary answered.

He said, "Call the police for me, Miss Blumenkopf. District Attorney's office, I guess. Tell them I have an Australian with me, name of Heysen."

"Sir?"

"Heysen. H-E-Y-S-E-N. He's going to make a statement. Call them now."

"Yes sir!"

I told him, "You don't want to know, do you, John? You're so tied to her you don't even dare to consider the truth." I stood up to leave. "I'm going to make you know it, John. It could be the only way out for me."

I backed out of his office. He sat there getting red in the face but he made no move to stop me.

His secretary was on the phone and she looked from me to the phone and back again, surprised. She stopped talking.

I started to move fast then, down the long corridor of empty offices, past the reception desk to the elevators. I punched the down button and waited impatiently, casting about for the stairs in case I needed them.

Nobody rushed out to stop me. The elevator arrived and slowly it descended and, as elevators always must at times like these, it seemed to stop on almost every floor and the passengers came slowly, casually aboard – one man held the door, loudly discussing his incomprehensible and certainly unimportant business with another before leaving – until finally the car was full and I was packed into the rear.

My fellow passengers emptied out ahead of me into the foyer. I had my coat over my arm and I walked out quietly and spotted the building security guard across the foyer, talking on the house phone, his eyes scanning the elevators.

He saw me. He said two words into the phone and started towards me. I ducked for the door.

"Excuse me . . . excuse me, sir . . . hey, *hey you!*"

But I was on Sixth Avenue and running through the traffic.

"Hey – hey there!" Three shrill blasts on a whistle. A cop on traffic duty. I kept running.

Word would get back to Detective Frank Pagnucco of the

D.A.'s office and now he would know for certain I was avoiding arrest.

I was on Sixth Avenue at 42nd Street and I sprinted for the subway entrance. A few cold people sitting quietly in a small park ignored me but I spotted a cop patrolling the park as he started in my direction.

My first reaction had been to get off the street and I had gone underground. But now I wasn't so sure. I was about to be cornered in the New York subway system and I had never been near it in my life.

Where did I buy a ticket? What destination should I give? A sign said *Tokens*. I gave the man a dollar and said nothing and he gave me six small brass tokens with some change and said nothing, and all the while I was glancing back over my shoulder. There was a line of turnstiles so I dropped a token into one and went through.

A tall Negro hurried past me. I followed him. I had no clue where he was headed but at least he was heading there fast.

I followed him out onto a gloomy platform and I was happy we had both been in a hurry; the train was about to leave. I slumped into a plastic seat and stared out onto the platform as we gathered speed and clattered into the tubular darkness of the tunnel.

"You look beat," Rose said when I finally stumbled into her apartment.

"I've been crawling around underground like a blind bloody pit pony," I said.

"You discovered our sweet-smelling subway transit system, huh?"

"It smells?" I asked. "I wouldn't have noticed. I've been switching trains all over. I was at 34th Street and then some place called Union Square and somehow I got up to 86th Street and had to risk a cab across town. Cunningham put the dogs onto me."

"Police?"

"None other. The city's finest."

"I hate to say it, Peter . . ."

"I know, Helga told me. He didn't want to hear. All I've done is alienate myself with him and put the police on their toes. They won't start a manhunt, I'm not important enough – hell, I haven't murdered anybody local yet – but a certain detective at the District Attorney's office will be hopping mad."

"What will you do?"

"I've got to get to Max Rolfe," I said. "He has to hoist me out of this mess. I'll call him on a pay phone at the hospital. If the cops do listen in they'd trace the call back here."

"Do you think this Rolfe guy can help, Peter?"

"He got me into it," I said.

"Yeah. If he got you into it . . . I can't see him getting you out of it."

Chapter 24

She was right.

"Hey," Rolfe said, "am I glad to hear from you! Listen, play it cool, they might be trying to trace your call."

"I can't imagine why."

"They've been with me all morning. I levelled with them, Pete, old friend. I told them all about Honolulu. I thought about it and figured if things have gotten so bad that you have to go into hiding in New York, then I better speak up."

"Generous of you," I said.

"Trouble is, it didn't help much. I'm being released from here tomorrow and they're escorting me back to Honolulu . . ."

"To face charges, I hope."

"It's not that simple. They can't find a single one of my prints in the entire hotel. They had a vague kind of description of a guy about my build and colouring entering the hotel but it was hazy and they didn't know for sure. You, it's different. They found fingerprints all over the rail of the terrace outside the room where the girl was killed."

"I didn't think they had any prints."

"They were badly blurred, it took them time to put all the pieces together then check them against the prints in your own hotel room. They still don't know for certain, but they're sure enough to want to talk with you. They figure I'm just trying to confuse them. You're the killer, you know they've almost convinced themselves of that? I couldn't say anything that would change their minds, old friend."

109

"I'll bet you tried hard, Max."

"Honolulu sent two of their investigating cops over here, they arrived yesterday and talked with me this morning."

"Thanks for your help, Max."

"I tried, Pete. Look, I'm sorry I got you into this, I thought you could bounce it off easy and we'd both be in the clear."

"Sure, Max. Do you know anything about the feller with the big ears, do you know him from anywhere in Elizabeth's past?"

"I wish I did, Pete. He hits hard. You haven't asked me how I am."

"Max – I don't care." I put the phone down and left the booth in a hurry, back to the comparative safety of Rose Meinrath's apartment.

She served up hash on toast for lunch and I ate it in silence, thinking. She tried to make conversation and finally gave up. She put coffee and a half-bottle of bourbon on the floor beside me and went out and left me alone.

Rolfe was a fool. He had put me in to save his own skin and then, relenting when he saw the trouble I was in, he had impetuously put himself in – but it no longer did me any good. They had my prints, near enough. They didn't have his. They had his admission that he had been in the hotel with Sandy Lee, an admission given freely. They had my admission of guilt by default; I had disappeared from my hotel, I had ducked arrest after talking with John Cunningham.

The coffee was hot and black and strong, and I took the bourbon as it came from the bottle.

Jug Ears. If I could find him, which was unlikely with the police seeking me, it wouldn't do me much good. Even if I beat a confession out of him it wouldn't hold up, he would simply deny it later. And he was clearly a man accomplished at covering his tracks.

John Cunningham was less than useful to me. He was a danger to himself, let alone a nuisance to me.

Elizabeth Cunningham was my only chance. It was Max Rolfe she wanted, not me. There was no reason why she shouldn't help me if I could show her a way to incriminate Rolfe. We had that much in common: as far as Elizabeth and I were concerned, they could hang Max Rolfe from the tallest palm tree.

The problem was, how to arrange it. However I looked at it,

110

Elizabeth Cunningham would have to willingly put her own head on the block and there was no way I could ever persuade a lady like Elizabeth Cunningham to discomfort herself for my freedom. From her point of view, her best play was to keep right out of it; she didn't care either way whether I was accused or not, so long as Max Rolfe was put away. Easiest way for her to achieve this was to say and do nothing.

I finished the coffee and made a large dent in the bourbon. I was beginning to like the stuff. I lay back on Rose's bed and smoked a cigarette and pondered the youthful beauty of Helga Brandt and the Machiavellian sweetness of Elizabeth Cunningham. And the ageing male stupidity of John Cunningham.

There was a way. It was risky but I had more than a vacation in jeopardy now.

I was still thinking about it when Rose returned and I had refined it some more in my mind when Helga arrived at the apartment. We sat over more coffee and I told them about it:

"It's an old American custom. If you can't get one of your leading gangsters for murder or fraud or whatever, you eventually get him for tax evasion."

"You will accuse Mrs. Cunningham of tax evasion?" Helga asked.

"She's probably guilty of that, too – but no. The point is, she was an accessory to the murder of that girl in Honolulu. She arranged it. But I can't prove it. So I'll hang another murder on her, one that I can prove."

"She killed someone else?" Rose asked. "She's a real sweetie, this Elizabeth Cunningham."

"It's not that she killed anybody else," I said, "it's that she's going to soon. Tonight, if possible, because we have to move fast."

"Elizabeth Cunningham is going to murder somebody tonight?"

"Certainly. She will attempt to kill her husband."

"Her husband?"

"I think it's a pretty fair assumption," I said, "that a man like John Cunningham would carry some hefty cover on his life. Elizabeth Cunningham is no stranger to life insurance, and tonight she will do in her old man, she'll try to kill him. I hope she won't succeed, but she'll try – and this time she'll have a witness."

"Witness?" Helga asked.

111

"You," I said. "Tonight you will see her make a deliberate and premeditated attempt on the life of her husband. John, of course, will survive the attack, but he will then be convinced that his wife is a killer. And isn't that all we want?"

Helga stared at me with big eyes. "I am a witness to a murder?"

"Yes."

Chapter 25

"Sounds a great theory," Rose said. "How does it work?"

"No bloodshed," I told them both. "It's very clean." I turned to Rose. "You work in a bar, you must meet a lot of people. Do you know any crooked doctors?"

She smiled. "Doesn't every girl on the West Side? What do you want, a phoney death certificate or something?"

"Drugs."

"Hell, that's easy."

"You put me up to it," I said. "Remember your story about the guy from Podunk, you convinced him he was poisoned? Happily for us, most wealthy old men take pills or potions of some kind – for their heart, their rheumatics or their sex – and Cunningham's no exception. That makes it too easy for Elizabeth to slip him an overdose of drugs. Helga will spot it and call Cunningham's own doctor, who will just manage to save the old man's life."

"It won't work," Rose said.

"Why not?"

"You couldn't feed an old man like him a fatal overdose of drugs and then just hope the doc makes it in time to pull him out of it."

"You're not following me," I said. "He doesn't in fact get an overdose. Well, not a *fatal* overdose. He only thinks he does. He gets enough to make him feel pretty bad. Helga, what's that stuff John Cunningham takes in his milk?"

"You mean at night? It is to make him sleep. His doctor says he does not sleep properly, he worries too much."

"Do you ever get it for him?"

"Oh no, only Elizabeth Cunningham gets it for him. She warms the milk and stirs it in every night."

"Always?"

"I have never seen him get it himself. If she is not home he does not care. I never do it. The drug is – I hear him call it chloral high-something."

"Chloral Hydrate?"

"That is it, yes."

"The insomniac's first friend. If he got an overdose he'd feel bad and you'd be there to help him. If you take the stuff regularly and then get an extra charge of it, you'd feel yourself going. He would have to believe Elizabeth had given him an extra belt of the stuff. She could deny it of course, but it wouldn't help her much."

"Then he would think she had tried to kill him. You have a horrible mind, Peter."

"I have to convince *someone* she's a killer. That, or I spend the rest of my days spooking around in the subway with my hat pulled over my eyes."

Helga said, "It will not work, Peter."

"Why not?"

"He always knows how much of his drug is there in the bottle."

"You mean he takes particular note of how much? He doesn't leave it entirely up to Elizabeth? It gets better, maybe he's a little scared already."

"But then to make him believe – after Mrs. Cunningham has made him his milk – you must remove the rest of the drug from the bottle."

"Toss it out the window, you're fourteen floors up, it'll never be found."

"Our apartment has full climate control, Peter. The windows do not open without much trouble. They are almost never open."

"Down the sink? It's easy. Here's what happens. You make sure there's just enough milk left for his nightcap, and no more. You mix something in the milk that'll react with the Chloral Hydrate to make him feel dopey and sick. It's up to Rose to find out what drug and how much of it – just enough to frighten him, make him feel bad without doing any real harm."

"That'll cost money, Pete."

"I should have enough on me, Rose. You, Helga, you wait in the kitchen – find some excuse to be there – and as soon as Elizabeth has warmed the milk and taken his nightcap to him, you tip the remainder of the drug in his usual bottle down the sink. How does your milk come, cartons or bottles?"

"We have it delivered in bottles."

"So you tip the drug down the sink and replace the drug bottle, then you wash out the milk bottle."

Rose looked worried. "Pete, there may be traces left in the pipes, in the u-bend thing under the sink . . ."

"Not if you wash it down well enough. If Helga gives the bottle a good workout and gets a lot of water flowing through the pipes, the police would have to perform surgery on the Manhattan sewers to find any trace of the drug."

"The police will be in this?" Helga asked.

I told her, "I think Elizabeth will be too worried about her chances of survival to call them in. But we'll have to get them in somehow, I'm hoping the doc will call them. If the cops suspect her of trying to do in John Cunningham, we can trade with her – Helga can go alibi for her in return for certain favours – like getting the two of us out of the mess we're in."

Rose said, "But Pete – if Helga is in the kitchen, this Cunningham woman can make her the number one suspect."

I thought about it. We were playing bluff and counter-bluff with Elizabeth Cunningham and right now our hands were equal. I needed to shuffle the cards and stack the deck to finish the game, but we had to be sure of the odds.

I said, "Where's your bedroom, Helga, is it upstairs with theirs?"

"Yes."

"Good. Forget the kitchen. You stay in your bedroom and make noises so both Elizabeth and particularly John Cunningham know you're there. John Cunningham has to be sure in his own mind that you never moved from there."

"I have a guitar."

"Play it loud. Let both the Cunninghams know that there's no way they could connect you with the drugs."

"But then who will empty the bottle and wash it away?"

"I will."

"But Peter . . ."

"You smuggle me into the apartment. You mix the extra

114

drug in the milk then go up to bed. As soon as Elizabeth follows with John Cunningham's milk, I'll get rid of the remainder of the drug in his regular bottle. You'll be completely in the clear. As far as anybody knows, Elizabeth will have been the only one in a position to do anything with his drug. And you'll be upstairs, closer to him and ready to help when the time comes."

Helga smiled. "Peter, it is very clever. But you do not know these big Manhattan apartment buildings. There is no way to smuggle you in without the doorman knowing, and if he knows then Mrs. Cunningham will know."

"There has to be some way in."

"No. I will tell you. Our building is not so different from the others like it. I do not mean here where we are now on the West Side. I mean an expensive apartment building on the East Side. There is a doorman on the door and he checks everybody in and out. You have seen him. Day and night there is a man at the door. If he goes away from the door he locks it and only the residents can get in with their own keys. We could wait all the day for the doorman to leave his door so I could unlock it and take you in."

"A back door, a trade entrance?"

"You know, we have closed circuit TV watching the only other entrance? It is always locked but it has closed circuit TV watching it, and all through the basement it watches always."

"You're joking!"

Rose said, "She's right, Pete. A lot of the fancy East Side places have it now. There is just no way into those big buildings without you pass the doorman."

"And then," Helga said, "you have to come out again because he has seen you go in."

I stared down into my empty coffee cup. "There has to be a way. If I can get in – and out again – without being seen, I can bring out with me the drug that Cunningham will think he's taken."

"Not that," Rose said. "If you're caught with that on you the game's over in the first innings. Put it down the sink."

"Sure, okay. But there's *got* to be a way into the place."

"I'll get more coffee," Rose said. "It looks like we're about to plan a murder."

Chapter 26

It was a little after four in the afternoon when Helga and I approached the apartment building. She gave me her key.

I waited half a block back for her to enter the building and as she disappeared inside I walked slowly towards the entrance.

When I reached the main glass doors there was no sign of Helga or of the doorman. The doors were locked. I used Helga's key and slipped quietly inside then locked the doors again.

Down a short corridor away from the entrance foyer, I could hear Helga talking with the doorman as he opened a security room; she told him there were some books in a trunk of hers that she needed right away. I pressed the elevator button and waited.

We needn't have worried. Helga kept him occupied helping to open her trunk and by the time he returned to the foyer I had reached the Cunninghams' floor, punched the elevator back to ground level, and let myself into their apartment. I left the door unlocked for Helga to follow.

They looked after the family servant pretty well in the Cunningham household; Helga's room was spacious, with wide windows and a view downtown across the rooftops of the nearest buildings.

In comparison with the rest of the apartment, however, her room was almost barren: a small bed, wardrobe, dressing table, some chairs and a desk, plain deep blue curtains against the white walls, and two pictures, both small abstract prints. There was an emptiness about the room, an impersonal quality that belonged more to a motel than a private room in a private home. It was as if she could toss all her belongings into a cardboard suitcase, throw a coat about her shoulders, and leave without a glance back. Perhaps she could.

I sprawled as comfortably as I could in one of the tightly stuffed blue lounge chairs and Helga brought me coffee.

She sat on the edge of her bed and looked at me. "It is the first time I have had a man in here."

"Do I seem out of place?"

116

She smiled. "Maybe I should have men in my room more times before this."

"You're joking, of course."

"Oh, there have been men, but I have always kept them out of here. Elizabeth Cunningham has a way of harming anything that gets near her. I do not want her to know too much."

"No special man, Helga?"

"Once . . . perhaps . . ." She gave a tiny European shrug. "I remember stupid little things. We had dinner at a place called La Toque Blanche on East 50th and ate *Quiche Lorraine* and drank white wine . . . and we walked home and he carried my shoes because it was so hot . . ." She shook her head to throw away the thought. "But I worry too much about myself, you see. I think too much about what will happen to me, I cannot relax."

"When this is over, Helga – come with me to Honolulu."

"I think you would rather take Elizabeth Cunningham with you."

"That was unfair."

"I know." She laughed. "I am bitter, I think you say. Perhaps I am jealous of her – of what she can do to a man like you."

"So come to Honolulu with me and relax."

"You said yourself, Peter – when this is over. Okay, when this is over we will see if you mean it."

I didn't answer her. But I did mean it. Elizabeth Cunningham had proved her own brand of witchcraft on me and had left me with every nerve jangling from her assault. But Helga had simply been Helga Brandt, cold and withdrawn on the surface yet with a warmth in her eyes that I wanted to investigate further. Somehow this was no place to make her understand how I felt.

And as if in answer to my thoughts, with the kind of feminine perception that can surprise a man, she crossed the room to take my cup and she placed her hand very briefly on top of mine. "Another time," she said softly. "Now we will have more coffee?"

Rose arrived at five. I went to the front door with Helga to let her in and we stood talking softly in the living room. Rose gave me a small screw-top bottle.

"It's harmless," she said, "but it fights with chloral hydrate to make you feel bad. He gave me just the right measure. You mix that lot with a glass of milk and his normal dose of chloral hydrate and he's going to be a sick old man."

I looked hard at her to read her expression and she caught my thoughts; she said, "We don't get guarantees, Pete. You can't be sure with these back-alley operators. He says even if Cunningham has a weak heart it shouldn't do him any real harm. But he also said he wouldn't remember anything about me if the cops came calling." She shrugged. "But quacks like him always say that."

Helga said, "It is a risk with an old man, Peter."

"Just how good is his health?" I asked her.

"He says it is very good. He is never sick. He takes his sleeping stuff and sometimes some iron pills for his blood but never anything else, not even aspirin."

"So it's a risk we have to take with him," I said.

Rose said, "If it backfires, Peter – if it really hurts him . . ."

"We're all in worse trouble."

All three of us stood there looking down at the innocent bottle in the palm of my hand. It might be freedom for Helga and myself. It might put us, and Rose, behind high stone walls for too long to contemplate. It might kill John Cunningham. We had only the word of a shady medico that it would not. Now we were face to face with it, we had a tough decision to make.

Helga made it for us. "I am frightened for us and for Mr. Cunningham," she said. "I like him very much. But Elizabeth Cunningham married him for his money, we know that. If he stays alive too long she will not be happy about that."

"On her past track record," I said, "Dear John could be Elizabeth's next victim."

"So," Helga said, "What we will do – it is necessary."

"Okay, come out to the kitchen, let's get this over."

There were two bottles of milk in the refrigerator, only one of them full. We tipped enough out of the half-empty one until it held no more than a glassfull. Then we mixed in the measure that Rose had brought us.

Helga hid the dosed milk in a high cupboard. When the evening meal was over, she would toss out all the other milk and replace it with the milk intended for John Cunningham.

Rose left hurriedly, taking the empty drug bottle with her. All we had to do now was make sure John Cunningham took his nightcap, then dispose of the remaining chloral hydrate, and Elizabeth Cunningham would be a murderess. It was too easy. Too easy.

I hid in Elizabeth's small sitting room, lying tight against the wall behind the settee. It was the only place to hide in the apartment. I had thought of joining the dogs or waiting in Helga's room but this was the only useful place for me. The waiting began.

I lay on the hard floor, quietly listening to the movement of the merry Cunningham household about their apartment; Elizabeth first, cursing the cold outside as she entered and wishing she could be in Mexico now as she had been at this time last year. She got ice from the kitchen and took it to the main living room, made a jugful of martini, and sat back to watch the news and grumble at the daily air pollution figures on TV.

John was next, murmuring his soft good evening to Elizabeth and then to Helga in the kitchen. Considerate, thoughtful Elizabeth hurried him into his chair and I heard her giving him his martini.

I listened to Helga preparing and serving the evening meal; the rattle of the plates and the gurgle of the water going down the sink. The gurgle . . . of the water . . . in the sink. That was going to be a lot of help.

The evening moved slowly. Their meal complete, John and Elizabeth Cunningham separated, John to go upstairs to his study, no doubt to tinker with a Confederate cannon or hone a good edge on a Cossack sword, Elizabeth to sit restlessly in the living room and read magazines.

Lying nervously on the floor in Elizabeth's sitting room, frustrated by the lack of action, I could hear Helga cleaning up in the kitchen and Elizabeth tearing through magazines, calling Helga for more coffee and then complaining because there wasn't enough sugar, then tearing through more magazines. It was good to know I wasn't the only restless one in the apartment.

Once, Helga came quietly to the door of the darkened room and spoke to me in a whisper. "They are both upstairs now," she said.

"I heard Elizabeth in there a while back, she sounded like she was eating back copies of *Vogue* and *McCalls*." I edged myself out of my bone-wrenching horizontal position and I could see Helga silhouetted against the light coming through the door, watching the staircase as she talked to me.

"She is worried," Helga said. "She does that when she is worried, she turns the pages over quickly and does not see them. Now she is in her room putting on her face."

"She's going out?"

"No. It is another thing she does. She always worries about her makeup. Some mornings she will wash it all off twice and do it again to get it right. When she is upset, she will sit at the dressing table and put her makeup on and take it off again. She will try it many ways before she gets tired of doing it. She has many oils and creams."

"Don't most women?"

"She has even more. It is an obsession."

"Come here, Helga."

"No. It would be better if I sit in the kitchen and read a book. It is a thing that I do."

"You're a happy little lot around here," I said. "He's playing with his private armory, she's rebuilding her face and you're sitting in the kitchen reading a book."

"I will go soon to my room and make bad noises on my guitar. Please be patient."

So I lay down again and ran it all over in my mind:

Elizabeth Cunningham, afraid her third husband was going broke, afraid Helga might one day put her in for being involved as a possible accessory to murder or at least for obstructing the course of a police investigation into her first husband's death, perhaps afraid of being somehow directly tied in with the deliberate and premeditated murder of an innocent Honolulu girl, was busily rubbing turtle oil and warthog's juice and extract of frogs' spawn collected by the full moon onto her face, maybe to erase the lines of fear and cynicism that must be there somewhere.

That same Elizabeth Cunningham was confident that she could use Helga's fear to her advantage, and that she could use her knowledge of her second husband's businesses to get herself out of any financial embarrassment she might be facing.

In her own room, Helga waited; afraid because she had no citizenship, virtually no legal existence; afraid that Elizabeth Cunningham could hand her over to the law to face, at very least, a charge of manslaughter.

Tonight she was even more afraid. Whether or not she had

killed in the past, tonight she would be an accomplice in another crime.

Upstairs in his study, John Cunningham, a pleasant enough man whose life work has slipped away from him, about to go bankrupt with the kind of honest pride that might have been admired in the days when he started work but now seemed ancient and sad. John Cunningham, totally captivated by a beautiful woman – maybe the first really beautiful woman he had had in his life – was right now unaware that this, I hoped, would be his last evening with her. I wished I could have arranged a little after-dinner pleasure for him before the blow fell.

And me, Peter Heysen, unknown here but too well known on the nation's TV screens at home, sought by the police for questioning, a murder suspect with no way to refute all the evidence pointing at me.

Elizabeth Cunningham had attempted to frame her second husband. Then he had framed me. Now it was only fair that I should frame her. It was very neat, very tidy, it completed the circle.

Tonight, if all went well, Elizabeth Cunningham would be accused of murder.

I rolled over to ease an aching hip then froze. I heard Elizabeth enter the kitchen.

Chapter 27

She carried her coffee cup out with her. I heard her moving about in the kitchen, putting the cup into the sink, getting a glass, taking the milk from the refrigerator, pouring it into a saucepan, putting the empty bottle in the sink; intensely listening to every sound I could piece together her actions.

Faintly, from upstairs, came the clumsy, dissonant sounds of Helga strumming her guitar. It's hard to make a guitar sound bad, but Helga could. I hoped she wouldn't want to take it to Honolulu with her.

I eased myself out from my cramped quarters behind her settee and walked over the soft carpet to the door. Helga had left it open by no more than a couple of inches. I peered through the crack and I could just pick out the light from the kitchen spilling into the dining area.

Finally the sound of her tipping the milk into a glass and stirring it reached me. I stepped back into the gloom and waited. She switched off the kitchen light and emerged, ready for bed in a long, flowing white nightdress. It was unfair to be dressed like that, giving a man chloral hydrate.

The instant she went out of sight up the stairs I edged the door open and moved lightly across the half-dark apartment into the kitchen.

I closed the kitchen door and switched on the light. I went straight to the shelf Helga had shown me, and took down John Cunningham's drug bottle. I took it to the sink and stopped dead. Elizabeth Cunningham had put her coffee things into the sink with the empty milk bottle and they lay there covered with water.

I listened and heard nothing above me. I had expected her to use the dishwasher but she had left those few small things in the sink and I cursed her laziness in not bothering to wash them out and empty the sink.

Waiting in Elizabeth's small sitting room I had heard the water gurgling and coughing down the plug hole. I knew that if I emptied the sink they would hear it upstairs. Even if I could find a way to do it silently, Elizabeth would sooner or later realise it had been emptied, and she would know immediately where the rest of John Cunningham's drug had gone. There was no way I could get rid of it.

John Cunningham, right now, would be taking his drug and unless I could dispose of the chloral hydrate in his bottle the game would be over.

I thought about taking it out of the apartment with me: that had to be the only way. Quickly I searched through cupboards, seeking a small bottle, a container, even a jar of jam into which I could pour the stuff . . . and then I stopped. Earlier, talking and planning the thing with Rose, she had pointed out the danger that lay in taking the drug from the apartment: if the doorman spotted me he would hand me to the police and they would search me and find the chloral hydrate and some bright cop would ask a few pertinent questions and before daybreak I would be strongly implicated in yet another unpleasant crime.

I couldn't take it out in my pocket. I couldn't leave it behind, lying around the apartment. And I couldn't dispose of it.

I stood in the kitchen, listening to Helga's guitar, and I tried to avoid thinking of the only possible answer. I didn't want to think about it but I finally had to do it:

I held the bottle with my handkerchief, to avoid leaving prints. Carefully I opened it. There was only one way to get it out of the apartment. I put the bottle to my lips and tipped it.

Slowly it trickled down my throat; sour and sticky. I couldn't simply carry it in my mouth and get rid of it later, there was too much of it. I gagged on it once and paused until it had passed, worrying about the noise. I tipped up the bottle once again and gradually drained it until it was completely empty.

I hadn't thought to find out from Rose Meinrath's quack just how much would be too much for me. It hadn't seemed important, we hadn't allowed for Elizabeth Cunningham's lousy housekeeping habits. It served me right: I had set it all up for John Cunningham to take an overdose and here I was doing the same thing, in fact probably consuming more of the stuff.

I wished I could wash away the stickiness of it in my mouth and throat but I wasn't game to turn on the tap for water.

Still using my handkerchief, I sealed the empty bottle and gently replaced it on the shelf. I switched off the kitchen lights and opened the door and moved again, more cautiously this time, back into the small sitting room.

How long, I wondered, could I last before the drug hit me? I had to get out of this place, well away from here before I could rid my stomach of the drug. But I couldn't leave right away. We had planned that I would have ample time to escape through the front foyer without the doorman spotting me, but I still had to wait for the opportunity.

I felt sick. Psychological, I told myself. But the knowledge that I had taken the stuff in large quantities was enough for me to almost sense it deep in my gut, oozing its way into my bloodstream. I held onto the door post and waited impatiently for things to happen.

There was always the risk that nothing would happen. Cunningham might not realise he had been slipped an overdose, he might simply go off to sleep if the two drugs didn't react as we expected. Helga was waiting in her room for a cry, a sound of alarm from Cunningham himself, any reason at all to give her the excuse to get to him.

The apartment was now completely still, save for Helga's guitar, and her style had deteriorated from bad to terrible. I could imagine her poised behind the closed door of her bedroom, nervously not even attempting to finger the right chords. The sound had a jarring, crashing quality that set a disturbing mood. I wondered how the other two could stand it: Elizabeth Cunningham in her own bedroom calmly preparing herself for sleep, and John Cunningham . . . what the hell *was* he doing right now?

Did he, perhaps, never really take the stuff at all, but get rid of it somehow every night?

No, it was a mad thought, my mind was getting away from me; I'd seen him drink it.

My legs were unsteady and I wanted to sit on the floor. It wouldn't be the drug yet, just the thought of the drug, that was doing it to me; but I had to wilfully prevent myself from sitting down.

What was keeping Cunningham, why didn't he yell out or fall over or something?

Was he all right up there? He wasn't a young man, it was a dangerous thing we were doing with his life. Necessary, as Helga had said, but dangerous. Was he, maybe, already dead?

He couldn't be. The drug was taking a long time to act because Rose's unfrocked back alley doctor had played it careful, he had given Rose a conservative dose – perhaps too conservative – probably the damn stuff wasn't going to affect him any more than his regular dose.

But that much, at least, went as planned. Just as I was feeling the cramps in my stomach and telling myself over again that it was all psychological, John Cunningham appeared silently at the top of the staircase.

I pulled back further into the shadows. I watched him. Slowly, deliberately, he began to walk down the stairs. Suddenly, robbed of his natural virility, he seemed an old man, groping for the energy to get to the bottom of the stairs.

Why don't you go and get Helga or Elizabeth? I thought. Why come down here? And as I saw him grasping for the bannister rail I also thought, What have we done to you, John

124

Cunningham? Wasn't one killing enough to have hanging over me, was I going to have to face trial for another one?

I wanted to run out to him, help him, get him to a doctor, make him bring up the drugs we had fed him. I told myself not to panic, he was a strong man even if he wasn't so young, and Rose's contact wouldn't have been fool enough to suggest too high a dose.

Where the hell was Helga? Wasn't she listening or watching for him?

Quietly, he continued down the stairs. He wasn't well at all; perhaps it was the angle of the light, but it seemed the lines on his face were more deeply etched, and for the first time since I had met him it appeared that his shoulders had the stoop of aged people.

He reached the bottom of the stairs, paused, and headed for the kitchen. Fascinated now, I watched him switch on the light and go into the room. I listened and heard him open a cupboard. And suddenly he broke the dreadful silence of the apartment:

"Helga! *Helga!*"

She must have been standing right by the door of her room. She was still dressed and she came down the stairs three at a time to the kitchen. I couldn't see them but I could hear their voices:

He told her, "This bottle. It's empty. Keep it. Don't lose it."

"Mr. Cunningham, you have had too much . . ."

"Full of the stuff. Have to be sick, get rid of it."

"The sink, Mr. Cunningham." And I heard the catch in her voice as she knew for the first time that I could not have tipped the drug down there. I heard her pull the plug and then I heard the sink empty and John Cunningham's feet shuffling on the kitchen floor as she helped him across the room.

Elizabeth Cunningham came to the top of the stairs and called down, "John, is that you?"

Helga answered, "It's Mr. Cunningham, he's sick."

I lost focus on Elizabeth for a moment as she hurried down the stairs. My God, I thought, that wasn't psychological; drug's working on me. When would I get out of here?

Helga knew what to do. I heard her making him sick. And then I heard his voice and I knew, if I could ever get out of here unseen, that we were winning:

125

"You gave me too much," he accused. "Goddammit, you gave me the whole bottle!"

"John!" I could almost see the look of horror on Elizabeth's face, I could sense the wheels already beginning to turn in her mind; she knew she hadn't done it, she would already be wondering how she could convince him.

Helga emerged from the kitchen. She went to the security phone and called the doorman.

"Gus, can you get up here quickly please, Mr. Cunningham is very sick. . . . Thank you, Gus, it is very urgent."

She put the intercom down and picked up the regular telephone and dialled a number. I knew she was calling John Cunningham's own doctor. She spoke to him briefly and put the phone down again, then looked up and saw me in the shadows of the sitting room. She gave me a quick, almost imperceptible nod and I knew that she at least was confident that Cunningham would be okay now.

Elizabeth came out of the kitchen and I lurched deeper into the darkness of the room.

"Helga, what are you doing?"

"I have called Doctor Roberts and also Gus to come and help."

"Doctor Roberts?"

"Of course. You gave him an overdose of his drug, he needs his doctor."

"How can you say that, Helga? Where's the bottle?"

"We will see when the doctor gets here."

"Why did you call the doorman?"

"Because I am afraid of you."

"Oh Helga, don't be a silly girl, there's bound to be a perfectly simple explanation."

"Excuse me, we must help Mr. Cunningham."

Elizabeth followed her back into the kitchen. Helga had played it well.

Clearly the doorman called Gus wasn't the speediest doorman in the city. All he had to do was lock the big entrance doors and come up in the elevator, but it seemed he took half my life to arrive.

By the time Helga let him in I had lost focus twice and I could feel my knees shaking with the effort of remaining upright. Or was it from fear of what I had done to myself? John Cunningham was in good hands, he was getting help and soon

126

his doctor would be here. I had to get out and even after that I couldn't expect much help.

Helga hurried the doorman into the kitchen. Now was my only chance, as we had planned it. I heard Helga trying to explain what had happened, and Elizabeth interjecting, arguing, telling Gus he wasn't needed.

I slid out of Elizabeth's sitting room into the main living room and heaved myself across it, glancing anxiously at the open door of the kitchen. John Cunningham was bent over the sink and the other three were clustered around him.

Helga had left the front door open and I all but fell out of the apartment into the waiting elevator.

As the elevator plunged downwards my stomach rose and I held firmly to the handrail around the interior of the elevator. As it braked to a halt my legs buckled under me and I fell to the floor. But I had to hurry now, I had to get a long way away from here.

The doors opened and I pulled myself up onto my feet. I paused long enough to press the button and send the elevator back up to the Cunninghams' floor, then stumbled out of it. I let myself out onto the street and slammed the entrance doors to lock them again.

The sudden, late night cold hit me hard and knocked me momentarily back into consciousness. The freezing air in my lungs gave me new strength. I reckoned I had enough energy to make Rose's apartment.

Chapter 28

Somehow I had to get across the park to the West Side. There were no cabs in sight and I knew that without a cab I would never reach Rose's apartment before I passed out.

I had to find a place, anyplace, where I could get water to drink, where I could safely and in peace rid my stomach of the chloral hydrate that was already seeping heavily into my system.

There was no point in heading across the park on foot; that

way, they would probably find me next morning under a tree with the squirrels. I knew I had seen a school around this part somewhere with a high wire fence around it; I reasoned that if I could get in there I could find water and make myself very sick in private.

I headed away from the park down one of the cross streets, dumbly searching for the school. I knew I was rolling about like a drunk, yet the cold night air definitely seemed to have cleared my head a little.

In the distance I could hear the howl of police sirens, and I thought, All I need now to complete the night is to be picked up by an eager cop who swears I'm drunk. The only other sound was the click of my heels on the pavement.

But that couldn't be right: I had rubber heels on my shoes.

I swung around and saw Jug Ears for the first time.

It occurred to me that he must camp outside the Cunningham apartment on an almost semi-permanent basis and I wondered why, and then I knew why: Elizabeth Cunningham was scared, she wanted him close because he was the one who had done her dirty work for her in Honolulu.

I saw him sitting at a table with a big girl from Utah and walking deliberately towards me in Central Park; he and Elizabeth Cunningham must have seen me as more of a threat than I had supposed.

I started to run and my feet were stupid, getting in the way of each other. I heard his shoes clicking behind me, trotting now, moving in slowly and cautiously like a dog herding cattle.

The fact that he had seen me leave the Cunningham apartment didn't bother me, that was simply his word against mine. But if he could hold me and prove that I was loaded with the drug that John Cunningham thought he had taken, then it would be all over.

I turned into Madison Avenue and there were strong lights ahead. Instinctively I veered towards them. Where there were lights there must be people, and where there were people there must be less chance of Jug Ears getting rough. I was feeling too tender all over for him to get rough with me right now.

The sign said MODERN AMERICAN SCULPTURE and under it in big red letters, BY PUBLIC REQUEST, OPEN TO MIDNITE EVERY NITE THIS WEEK.

I looked up and the building was falling out over me. The place appeared to be surrounded by some kind of dry moat with a cat-walk across it. Inside there were lights and people and movement.

Another sign said, WHITNEY MUSEUM OF AMERICAN ART.

I ran inside and the sudden strong lights and warm air stopped me. My head slumped forward and I raised it slowly, with effort, and saw faces staring at me. I heard the steady clicking of heels as he followed me into the place.

There had to be a back entrance. I stiffened myself, standing up very straight, and followed a small group into an elevator. The doors closed as I saw Jug Ears enter the foyer and catch sight of me.

The elevator dropped us all off at another floor and I walked out of it, still very erect, and I knew I was going out of my mind: huge wings of stainless steel slowly flapped over my head across the ceiling and a beast in primary colours with six bright green horns growing out of its face squatted and stared at me; a wall of black cubes to my right, and to my left a massive structure of curving aluminium arms beckoned for me to crawl inside it and die. A geometric gnome blinked at me. Beyond it there were stairs. Jug Ears would probably come up those stairs.

"Excuse me, sir."

He was a guard, he wore a uniform but no gun. His expression said he knew I was high on something and whatever it was I had to go, and I didn't wait for his invitation. The elevator doors were closing and I stumbled back into it.

The elevator was huge, like a cavern, and it was going down and I knew what was going to happen but there was nothing I could do about it; as it braked my legs folded up under me like a collapsible chair. My mouth tasted carpet. I reflected that the carpet was a very nice shade of blue.

Somebody was helping me to my feet. It was very kind of them. I raised my head and saw Jug Ears only two feet away from my face. I shook my head and wrenched myself free of the arms holding me and I was going down again, down into a frightening world of abstract monsters with stainless steel wings and black enamel legs.

"He's my friend. He has this condition."

And it's a pretty poor condition, I told myself. Who spoke just then? Friend or foe?

"You can see he's not drunk, you just smell his breath."

129

The voice kept washing over me and it felt good. I thought I might just lie down and let it happen.

"If you could just get me a cab, I'll take him to his regular doctor."

"Are you sure, Ma'am? He looks like some kind of junkie to me."

Yes, I thought, I'm a raving, screaming drug addict. A dope fiend! Get high and rape your daughters! But all I want now is sleep.

"He's schizophrenic. You know, schizophrenia? He gets real violent sometimes. He needs his regular doctor to give him his shots, otherwise he has these fits, he breaks out all over like a crazy man."

"I'll help you get a cab for him, Ma'am."

"Here, let me help."

That last was Jug Ears's voice: I stopped falling, I stopped breathing.

"No thanks, strangers get him mad. If he's with me, he's okay."

I started breathing again. I saw lights, a big yellow car, and we were being carried along, my head in her lap, her hand stroking my brow and I liked that but I was wet through with sweat. Cold air rushed at me through the window of the cab and I opened my eyes and saw Rose, and then her face disintegrated into tiny blobs of colour out of focus.

We were going up steps and then there was just the two of us in the bathroom and it was going to be all right. I had never been so wretchedly sick but I didn't care now. I felt her strong hands tearing my clothes off and I thought, how's that for kicks, and I felt water and it was cold and tasted good on my tongue.

Then there was only softness, a soft bed, a soft pillow, and all I wanted was sleep.

I woke up suddenly and felt her beside me but when I opened my eyes I saw blonde hair and blue eyes and Helga said, "You were shivering and calling out so I am in bed with you to keep you calm."

"Come to Honolulu with me?"

"Yes."

Slowly I became more aware of her beside me and we made love gently and then she lay back beside me again and said, "You recover very quickly, don't you?" She started to say something else but I was asleep.

130

Chapter 29

"That was quite a night you had," Rose said.

I sat up in bed slowly and she gave me black coffee. She took another look at me and came back with three pills and a glass of water. I held them and glanced up at her.

"Excedrin," she said, "for your hangover. It's the age of drugs we live in."

"I think I'll just stay with black coffee."

"Suit yourself." She took the pills away again. "How do you feel?"

"I've got a sore back."

"Yeah, I dropped you on the bathroom floor. Maybe I broke your spine?"

"Was I pretty bad, Rose?"

"Well, you took a real belt of that stuff. Helga told me about it."

"Where is she now?"

"She's out buying you a new shirt and some underclothes. I got kinda rough when I stripped you for bed." She grinned. "It's not every lady gets to tear the shorts off a man. Helga should be back in fifteen. Listen, you better be good to that girl. She was pretty upset last night, she needed you."

I nodded. We had needed each other.

"How did you find me, Rose?"

"I didn't go to work. I figured I should stay close."

"Where were you?"

"I walked up and down Fifth Avenue like I was in business there. It was a cold night but you know something, I could've been in business anyway? Boy, the men who came up to me!"

"Did you see Jug Ears?"

"He must've been sitting there all the time in a parked car. I didn't see him. I was two blocks away, just walking, when you came out of that place like it was New Year's or something. I saw you roll down 75th Street and then I spotted your buddy with the Dumbo ears coming after you. I lost you in the Whitney but then I found you taking a nap in the elevator. The guard wanted to call the cops."

131

"I remember that part. You said I was going to throw a fit."

"Yeah. I never knew anybody get a cab for a lady that fast."

"Did Jug Ears follow you?"

"No chance. By the time he'd gotten his car or another cab, we'd have been out of sight."

"What about Cunningham?"

"He wasn't too bad. Scared some, but not as sick as you, by all accounts. Helga says his doctor put him under observation in hospital."

"And he's okay?"

"Sure, sure. Relax, it worked. Helga says he right off blamed his wife for it. Just like you said he would."

"The doctor called the police?"

"Well, no. It seems old Cunningham persuaded his doctor he shouldn't do anything, he should just sit pat."

"What about the doorman, he didn't call the police?"

"You know that doorman, he's right in with Mrs. Cunningham. She's a big tipper."

"So she's still loose? And Jug Ears too?"

"Look, relax, Pete! Everybody's okay. Helga doesn't think Cunningham is going to call in the police, you know how he's hooked on his wife. He believes she tried to kill him but he's a funny guy, he didn't want the police involved, he'll handle her his own way, I guess."

"Wouldn't the hospital report a patient if they suspected suicide, an overdose of drugs . . . ?"

"I guess his doctor persuaded them to cool it. I mean, he's a big name. It's a good hospital but they're human, they don't want to make trouble for people."

"Rose, that doesn't help me and it doesn't help Helga. The police have to be involved, otherwise Helga can't offer to go alibi for her. Don't you see? She has to be in trouble so we can trade with her."

"Well she's sure as hell in no trouble with the police, Pete."

"Is she still at the apartment?"

"I guess so. After they took Cunningham to the hospital she started in on Helga, she got real tough, she knew she'd been set up but she couldn't prove anything. Helga got out and came around here." She smiled. "Me, I had a miserable night on the floor."

I put the coffee down. "I've got to see Elizabeth Cunningham," I said. "She still holds the advantage over Helga and me."

"Will you do something for me, Pete?"

"What's that?"

"Don't stand up yet. Wait till Helga gets back here with your shorts?"

Chapter 30

The doorman stopped me. "I want to see Mrs. Cunningham," I told him. "My name's Heysen."

He called her on the security phone and I could hear her voice from where I stood: "Tell him *no!*"

"I'm sorry sir, I guess Mrs. Cunningham just isn't in to . . ."

"Call her again and tell her I'm on my way to the District Attorney's office. I just wanted to know if there was anything she wanted me to tell them."

He looked at me coolly. His face said he had seen everything in his life as a doorman. He picked up the security phone again and reported to her. This time her voice was calmer.

The doorman told me, "You can go right up, Mr. Heysen."

"Thanks."

She was waiting for me with the door open. She had pulled on orange slacks and a blue jumper but she had no makeup and her hair had only been roughly combed out. She was smoking.

"What's this business with the D.A.?"

"Do you mind if I come in, Elizabeth?"

"Come in, come in." She slammed the door hard behind me. "How did you do it, Heysen?"

"Do what?"

"I think 'patsy' is the term, isn't it?"

"Elizabeth, I heard John was sick and I called around to . . ."

"You know what I'm talking about."

She paced across the room and stubbed out her cigarette. The ashtray had a few butts in it.

"Okay," I told her, "I heard you tried to kill John last night.

133

Overdose of drugs. You admitted you set up Max Rolfe and then he set me up. Now you're in trouble yourself."

"Neat," she said. "How did you fix it?"

"I didn't say I had anything to do with it, Elizabeth." I sat down and watched her move across the room, a lean package of slow-burning energy. "My hands are as clean as yours are," I told her. "Is John calling the police?"

She stopped and grinned at me. "That's where you goofed, Peter Heysen. I went to see John in the hospital this morning. Oh, he believes I tried to knock him out, you succeeded that much. But he's not going to get the police in. I'm free to leave, anytime."

"He sent you packing?"

"He's giving me money and sending me away. I'm mad about that, Heysen. The score isn't even, not by a long shot. And you haven't helped yourself get free of that Honolulu business..."

"Yes I have," I told her. "All I need do is call the District Attorney's office, I know a man there, and tell him you tried to kill your husband. An allegation is made, they've got to investigate it. Most likely they'd start with the hospital and no hospital authorities are going to play silent when there's an investigation. Then it won't matter what John says, the police will still have to charge you."

She sat down and crossed her long legs. She lit another cigarette and watched me, visibly calming herself. "It looks like stalemate again," she said slowly. "You won't put me in because you know I could put Helga in."

"Elizabeth, the way things are now, you have to fear her more than she fears you. If they re-opened the inquiry into Bonifacio's death and found her not guilty – which is a fair possibility – the worst she'd get is a deportation order. But you, Elizabeth, deliberately and maliciously gave your husband an overdose of his sleeping drug."

"But I didn't succeed. And if John won't turn me over to the police now, he's certainly not going to appear for the prosecution if you turn me in, is he?" She smiled – a stiff little smile, a scared smile – and she stood up to pace the room again.

"You see, Peter Heysen, if you call in the police, maybe they won't charge me. You know I didn't do it. Maybe I could convince them, who knows? You can't bank on it."

"It's a reasonable risk."

134

But she ignored me, it was as if she was thinking out aloud. "If you call them in, I'll tell them I think you had some part in it. They won't take too much notice of you – and you couldn't expect me to help you, could you ?"

I was silent at that, wondering at this incredible, constantly shifting poker game we were playing, tossing about in my mind for an ace or even a lowly deuce that might tip the cards in my favour.

She went on, "In other words, if you follow up your threat, both you and Helga will have to face some kind of trouble one way or another. And I just *might* get off! At worst, I'd get a light sentence. You can imagine how I'd play the scene in the courtroom, can't you, especially as my own husband won't appear against me ?"

"Frail and tearful," I said. "It was a terrible accident and you still love him dearly . . ."

"Exactly."

"Only one thing wrong."

"What's that ?" she asked.

"You don't ever want it to come to a courtroom, do you, Elizabeth ? All the scandal ? You might have your little revenge on Helga and me, but that wouldn't compensate you for having to stand up in that court. And I think the odds are that you would have to do time. You wouldn't like that, either."

"Don't try to call my bluff, Peter."

"I'm sorry, Elizabeth, but I have to." I stood and went to the phone. I picked up the Manhattan directory from its shelf under the phone and looked up the District Attorney's number. I took my time looking, I took my time dialling, and I didn't look at Elizabeth. They took no time to answer.

"I wish to report a crime," I said, but I didn't get any further. Elizabeth came up behind me and put her hand on the phone, cutting off the call. Her eyes were steady and cold. She took the handset from me and replaced it on its cradle. "Peter Heysen," she said, "let's discuss business."

"That's much better."

"My freedom for yours, okay ?"

"And Helga's," I said.

"All right." She sat down and motioned me to a chair. "The man who attacked you last night is the man who killed the girl in Honolulu."

"Jug Ears," I said.

"I suppose you could call him that. His real name is Henry Datzek."

"Tell me about him, Elizabeth."

"I knew him in high school," she said. "A long time ago. He always wanted me but I never let him have me. A girl had to know what she was worth in that town." She lit a cigarette and her eyes never left me. "One night he was bringing me home from the high school dance and he was high on booze and all over me, and there was a hit-run accident. The man didn't die but he was in bad shape for a while and I think he lost a leg or something like that. I don't know why I never said anything. I suppose I just didn't want to get mixed up in anything. But Henry Datzek thought I did it for him."

"And you let him go on thinking that?"

She tossed her long hair away from her face. "It wasn't the gentlest neighbourhood. A girl did what she could to get by. I saw Henry again three years ago. Or I guess I should say he saw me, right on the street here in New York. He was broke, he was tied up with the loan sharks, and he wanted help. I gave him money, got him out of trouble, made him dress a little smarter. I helped him like he said he wanted."

"And then you made him earn it, right?"

"He didn't want to do it at first."

"But you worked on him."

"Yes."

"You reminded him of the hit-run accident."

"Yes. And he'd always wanted me so I finally let him, now and then."

"You're very good at that kind of thing. But he wasn't too good at his end of the deal."

"No, he goofed in London, so I sent him to Honolulu. He paid that girl to work on Max and get him up to the hotel room. She didn't know why, of course. Henry was there all the time, waiting on the terrace."

"What about the other girl, the one I was with?"

"He didn't know those two were friends and worked together. He didn't know Max would call you and pass the buck."

"Where do I find Henry?" I asked her.

"If I give you Henry Datzek, will you let me go free?"

I lit a cigarette myself then. I inhaled deeply.

She said, "John is letting me go. He wants me out of the apartment by the time he gets away from the hospital. He's giving me money and he'll divorce me quietly in Mexico. No scandal. If you don't stand in my way, Henry Datzek will take the rap for killing the girl in Honolulu – and as a small bonus, I won't say anything to anyone about Helga."

"How can you be sure Datzek won't incriminate you, Elizabeth ?"

"Henry won't do that."

"You really have a way with the boys, don't you ?"

"It does seem that way, doesn't it ?"

"And how do I know Datzek will confess ?"

"Making him confess is your problem," she said. "I'm sure you have a way with the boys too, Peter."

Chapter 31

Now it was perfectly simple: all I had to do was punch Henry Datzek in the chops a few times and he would write out his confession just like that, and he would conveniently keep my name and Elizabeth's name out of it. Poor, simple Jug Ears.

Poor, simple Heysen.

Datzek was not, as Elizabeth had predicted, waiting down below in any of the parked cars. I tried his apartment.

He lived on the East Side, on 89th Street, in a gloomy old brownstone. Here there was no doorman, no closed-circuit TV in the basement, just a regulation fat old lady peering out of a street-level window.

"I'm looking for Mr. Datzek."

"Who wants him ?"

"Friend of a good friend."

"Second floor, apartment 2B."

I knocked on his door. The peephole clicked as he opened it and looked at me through the lens. I noticed it was the only peephole in the building, he must have fitted it himself. I stood where he could easily see my face.

I heard the lock snap back and as he eased the door open I pushed it all the way, throwing myself to one side while grabbing for his wrists. I had expected him to be holding a gun or a knife but his hands were bare and he backed off smartly. He was quick on his feet, I knew that much about him already.

I kicked the door shut behind me. The apartment was big, it seemed, with scant furniture, and newly painted white walls and ceiling.

He continued to back off and I moved in quickly. I grabbed for his shirtfront and almost as if he had expected the move he wrapped his hand around my arm and pulled and twisted and I knew something else for certain now as I went over: he had taken more than six lessons in the old Japanese arts.

With reflex alone I managed somehow to come down feet first and wrench myself around to throw a hard punch up into his gut. The muscles there were firm and strong and he didn't flinch much. I saw his karate chop coming and I swung up fast, deflecting it with my arm and landing my knee in his gut at the same time.

That felt better, it went in good and deep and winded him. He knew something now: I was a dirty fighter.

So was he. He tried the old knee jolt himself and it bounced off my hip with a crack that was going to give me a lot of pain later when I stiffened up, I knew that already. I grabbed his knee as it came up a second time and I kept it coming, up and over with an assist from a toe in the sub-umbilical area, and that felt better still.

I stepped away from him and he lay on the floor looking at me; it had all taken a matter of seconds.

"I reckon I owe you another round," I said out of sheer bravado and I wished I hadn't said it. His feet snapped out and scissored under my knees and down I went as he came up at me. I threw my foot at him but this time it missed its primary target. He tried to duck under it and I crashed the heel of my shoe into his throat. He went down hard for the count as I got to my knees and slowly to my feet.

I crossed the big room to the window and leaned my back against the sill. "I guess two rounds will do me for now," I said. It was about all I could take. I felt my hip. Yes, it was going to be very blue and sore. So was his throat.

Nursing himself now, he slumped into an old settee against the wall. He lit a cigarette and coughed and ground it out under his foot on the wooden floor.

He looked up at me. "What do you want?"

"I want you to talk to the police."

"Name a good reason."

"I've just been with your friend Elizabeth. It's all over, Datzek."

"She's in trouble, I'm not."

"The only way for her to get out of trouble is for you to go to the police."

"You still haven't named one good reason why I should."

I moved towards him. He said, "You might not last a third round."

He was right, of course. Already I could feel the blood pounding in my head and I knew I still wasn't too good after the previous night's engagement with John Cunningham's drug.

"If I talk to the police," he said, "I take her with me."

I could see it starting all over again. If Datzek put Elizabeth in, she would put Helga and me in, the police would have a field day, and at least one nearly innocent person – namely, Peter Heysen – would go to jail for a crime he didn't commit. Perhaps I could take Max Rolfe with me and we could all go to jail together.

"Heysen," he said, "You set her up somehow, I don't know how, and even if I do guess I can't say anything to the cops without putting myself on the line. I talked to her this morning early, I know old Cunningham is giving her the push. She's no use to me anymore, the game's blown, you can see she's downhill all the way now. Why should I protect her?"

I lit myself a cigarette and stared at Datzek through the smoke. I tried to imagine him with Elizabeth. They both sickened me. I wished I had gone to New Zealand or Tasmania for a vacation. All I wanted was to get out of this city, to get to some place that was clean and warm and fresh, to take Helga with me and relax and not have to think.

"Come with me," I said. "Come and we'll talk with Elizabeth, perhaps she can persuade you."

He stood up, smiling. "That I could almost enjoy," he said.

Chapter 32

"Ridiculous!" Elizabeth screamed. She strode up to Datzek and slapped him hard in the face.

He grinned. "That won't work, Elizabeth."

She collapsed into a chair, one of her legs folded under her. "Henry, Henry . . ." she said.

"That won't work either."

She looked up at him. "We had a good thing going for both of us, Henry."

"Yeah. Till you let this guy frame you. He framed you so good you can all but see how he did it and you still can't do anything about it. You loused it up. I told you, I'm not taking the rap for both of us. If I go, you go."

"Henry," she said, "name it. Anything you want." Her voice was soft now and close to pleading. "I still have contacts, good friends, we could find you the smartest criminal lawyer in the city. What's the name of that lawyer who's always getting hoods off on technicalities? I'm not broke yet, Henry."

"It's not enough, Elizabeth."

"Goddammit, there must be something! Peter there is about to pick up the phone and have us all in court together if you and I can't decide how to get him off this dreadful Honolulu thing. Isn't there anything? Isn't there *anything*?"

"I just can't take you to jail with me, Elizabeth."

It came to me as he said that, and I stood up. I had found the last twist of the knife and as I looked at Henry Datzek I knew he would accept it.

"You can't take her with you, Henry," I told him, "but there may be another way. It's second best but it's not bad."

"How's that?"

I spoke to Elizabeth. "Whichever way you look at it, Elizabeth, Henry has the drop on you. And he thinks of you both as a team, so why not keep it that way? Make him a real offer. Tell him you'll keep the team in business."

Both of them watched me, neither catching the drift, so I spelled it out for them, enjoying every moment:

"Elizabeth, you put up the money for the country's best

criminal attorney for Henry. You have to anyway, because if Henry isn't satisfied he can always name you as an accessory. I presume he can prove it?"

He nodded. "Almost my whole income is in personal checks drawn on her account. All they need do is ask my bank. If I can prove I was on their payroll, the cops can take it from there and find out why without much effort."

"Good. So much for the present, now for the future. Some time soon, Elizabeth, John will divorce you. When Henry has served his term, you marry him. It's perfectly . . ."

"No!"

But Henry Datzek was smiling as I had predicted he would.

"Henry," I said, "is a nasty, vicious little bastard, and you're a cold, grafting bitch. But Henry likes you. You have to go along with him if he wants it that way. At any date, now or in the future, Henry merely has to call in the police and tell them a few things about you and you'll go inside. What do you think, Henry?"

He laughed. It was a cruel laugh. "I like it," he said. "For that, I'll take the rap. When I get out she'll keep her end of the bargain."

Elizabeth swayed in her chair. She knew she couldn't escape it; she was trapped by her own game, by her own miserable hatchet man. Her flesh was pale and I was sorry she hadn't put on any makeup. Even her nervous habit of doing her face when she was disturbed seemed to have deserted her. Gradually she emerged from her nightmare thoughts.

"You," she told me, "I should have let the dogs at you . . ."

"It's kind of poetic," I said. "It all started with you using Datzek to frame Max Rolfe, who framed me, so I brought Datzek back to you and you repay him in the nicest possible way. I'd like to wish the bride and groom every happiness." I looked at my watch. "That's what I call making the punishment fit the crime. Do you need time to decide, Elizabeth?"

She lowered her eyes. "No."

"All right, Henry," I said, "The District Attorney's office is only a short ride away. At least you have something to look forward to while you're inside."

He laughed some more. He was a happy man. "It's a deal?" he asked Elizabeth.

"A deal, Henry." She slowly looked up at him.

"Come on, Henry," I said, "one of us gloating is enough."

We went to the door and I stopped and glanced back at Elizabeth Cunningham, the glamorous Elizabeth Cunningham, slumped in her chair. She saw me and she sat up straighter and some of the old fire and glitter came back into her eyes.

"And you, Peter Heysen," she said. "You. I'll see you again. One day. Somewhere."

I believed her. That final, bitter expression in her eyes would stay with me. It also told me I certainly hadn't seen the last of her.

One day. Somewhere. It wasn't a comfortable thought.

I took Henry Datzek to the District Attorney's office.

Chapter 33

"Questions and more questions," I told Max. "I thought I'd never shake myself free of New York."

The three of us – Helga, Max Rolfe and myself – had spread ourselves beside the hotel pool, cold drinks within reach and the warm sun all around us.

"I said I owed you, Peter. How about it ? What can I do for you, how can I apologise, how can I thank you ? Isn't there anything ?"

"Max, you won't understand, but please don't ask me that question again. I mean it."

"You're sure there isn't anything ?"

I smiled at him warmly, I felt genuinely warm towards him. I told him, "Max, you'll repay me one day, I'm sure of it."

Max Rolfe thought he had talked his way into the clear. What I had neglected to tell him was that I was certainly in the clear because I had brought them Datzek. My release in return for Datzek was a fair exchange, though it had taken some serious negotiating. But on the other hand, a recommendation had gone to the Justice Department to have Max Rolfe charged with obstructing due process and withholding vital information and other similar wrongs that carried considerable penalties. That had not taken quite so much negotiating. I was able, then, to smile at Max with real warmth and fellowship. They would be calling for him in a day or so.

"Okay, if that's the way you want it," he said. "Thanks anyway." He turned to Helga. "Main problem right now is getting papers for Helga. Maybe we should marry her off to some all-American boy, that should make citizenship easier."

She laughed, lightly and happily. She was a new person: alive and suddenly very beautiful. Especially when she looked at Max Rolfe.

We watched him dive into the pool and strike out down its length.

"He was always a good swimmer," Helga said.

"You're pretty keen for him, aren't you?"

She looked at me quickly, then away. "I am a silly girl, Peter. I have been living too long inside myself, I have many feelings I do not understand. It is different now I see him again – and she is not here."

"I'm supposed to leave tomorrow," I told her. "I've got to be back in Sydney to prepare for the new show." And I watched her eyes as I told her, "But I could always break my contract and stay here and help you."

Her eyes had never left Max Rolfe. She didn't even look at me as she said, "That is not necessary, Peter."

And as Max Rolfe clambered out of the pool and approached us, laughing, I told myself: Peter Heysen, the world is full of bastards, and you need to be as illigitimate as the rest in order to survive. And yet I had the feeling that I had just died in Honolulu.

AN AMERICAN DREAM 5/–

Norman Mailer

Author of *The Naked and the Dead*

There is nothing insubstantial or fairylike
about *An American Dream*. It is a great
powerhouse of a novel; a masterpiece of brutal
realism; a blend of raw sex and tender love,
hate and brutality, Good and Evil, with all the
terrifying tension and pent-up violence of an
awakening volcano.

With *An American Dream* Mailer reaffirms
his towering stature as a novelist. Using the
framework of a first-rate detective story,
he has created much more—an epic of our own
time, a triumphant return to the greatness
which made *The Naked and the Dead* the
outstanding novel of World War II.